Afghan Stories

Oleg Yermakov
Afghan Stories

Translated from the Russian by Marc Romano

Originally published in Russian in diverse magazines

First collected in France, by Editions Albin Michel, as *Contes Afghanes*

First published in Great Britain in 1993

by Martin Secker & Warburg Limited

an imprint of Reed Consumer Books Ltd

Michelin House, 81 Fulham Road, London SW3 6RB

and Auckland, Melbourne, Singapore and Toronto

Published with the permission of Editions Albin Michel, S.A.,

22 Rue Huyghens, 75014 Paris.

A CIP catalogue record for this book

is available from the British Library

ISBN 0 436 20127 5

Phototypeset in 12/15 Perpetua by Wilmaset Ltd, Birkenhead, Wirral

Printed in Great Britain by

Mackays of Chatham PLC, Chatham, Kent.

Contents

Baptism 1

Unit N Carried Out Exercises 26

Mars and the Soldier 37

Winter in Afghanistan 43

The Belles 70

The Snow-Covered House 85

A Springtime Walk 98

A Feast on the Bank of a Violet River 114

Safe Return 140

The Yellow Mountain 161

Baptism

The reconnaissance company left the camp at night. Headlamps out, its BMPs rolled northward. The lights of the camp quickly disappeared, and the infinite warm spring night engulfed the column.

The soldiers riding on top of the caterpillar-tracked machines were looking at the dense trails of constellations above them. Kostomygin was staring up at the shining trails too, and thinking that the rumble of their engines could probably be heard in the remotest *kishlak* on the farthest end of the steppe, assuming, of course, that it had an end . . .

Half an hour later a dull moon appeared low over the steppe. The moon slowly rose, the night brightened, and the outline of scrubby hills began to show against an expanse of black and white.

Straight ahead, white walls and towers were becoming distinct. The column was rapidly drawing nearer to a *kishlak*.

'Okay, stay awake!' the captain said into the radio microphone he was holding to his throat. The commander of each BMP heard the message and one after the other reported in: number so-and-so, I read you. The BMP guns swung left and right, and the soldiers reached for their assault rifles and began to stir.

The column tore through the *kishlak* without slowing down, but nothing happened.

Kostomygin managed to spot dark slits on the towers, houses with flat roofs, lush gardens behind *duvals*, the long-eared silhouette of a donkey next to a barn.

Beyond the *kishlak*, the road – it was now easy to make out – led down an incline and crossed a shimmering river. Still at the same speed, the machines forged through the wide, shallow waters and pressed onwards.

Kostomygin had gulped down the fragrant air of the *kishlak*'s flowery gardens, and now there was a sweetness in his mouth. He bared his face to the warm wind, sensed the weight of his ammo pouch against his side, felt the tightness of his short, laced boots, the lightness and freedom of his camouflage gear, and all of it pleased him: this moon, this terrible steppe, the flowery sweetness in his mouth, his comfortable uniform, the weapon across his chest, the speed of these powerful machines through the endless black-and-white plains under bright and alien constellations.

The column came to a halt on a ridge between two low hills. The soldiers clambered down from the machines and stretched their legs.

They fell in in column and began to march along the road. The drivers and mechanics stayed with their machines.

The company moved through the hills. Everyone was silent, sullenly looking around at the surrounding hilltops, which were clearly outlined against a backdrop of stars. The moon had sailed across to the western edge of the sky, then turned the colour of bronze, and was already shining less brightly than before.

A few steps behind him Kostomygin heard Oparin, like him a

green kid, jangling his belt buckle while trying to pull the stopper from his canteen. There was a thud and Oparin hurtled forward into him. Kostomygin spun around to face him. Hastily replacing his canteen on his belt, his head hunched into his shoulders, Oparin resumed the march. Directly behind him, striding briskly, was Shvarev, a tall long-legged sergeant.

Have to watch out, Kostomygin thought to himself, turning away.

The sparrows – men who'd served more than six months – often warned the kids to keep on their toes and do everything they were told. Any mistake a kid made during an operation, they said, would be 'investigated' by the veterans once they got back to camp. A reconnaissance company wasn't an artillery unit or an infantry or an engineer battalion; everyone had to be 'on the ball', everyone had to be at least as good as any 'beret'.

After a month's service, Kostomygin had seen enough old-timers' hearings for his tastes, and under no circumstances did he want to be among the accused at the next one. And here was Oparin already on the black list. He'd have to stay alert.

The moon vanished, the steppe became dark once more, and the stars began to shine more brilliantly. The company was marching rhythmically along the hills.

The night had cooled off. A bird whistled from the steppe.

Footfalls could be heard directly ahead.

'Hurry!' Shvarev ordered in a loud whisper, and Kostomygin broke into a run. We're too late, he thought to himself.

They ran for ages, sweating, swallowing dust.

Kostomygin was clutching his assault rifle in one hand and his canteen in the other, but his magazine-filled ammo pouch was pounding him brutally in the ribs, so he let go of his rifle and grabbed the pouch instead. But the rifle banging against his chest was even more painful and he grabbed for it again.

They ran so hard and for so long that Kostomygin's breath started to come out in rasps, and he swore that he would never again, not in a million years, touch a cigarette.

Finally they reached the very last hill and spotted the silhouettes of towers, houses, and *duvals* on the steppe below. The wind was blowing from the *kishlak*, and Kostomygin caught the same gentle aroma of flowers. The wind picked up strength, and a powerful flowery wave cascaded over the panting, dust-covered men in their soggy and acrid-smelling clothes.

At the base of the next hill there was a fork. One road, the road they had been running along, led to the *kishlak*; the other wound down to the steppe. Two platoons, under the command of the captain and a lieutenant, moved off towards the *kishlak*; the rest of the company lay low on the hill, taking cover behind boulders and training their light machine-guns and assault rifles on the fork.

Kostomygin carefully lowered himself against the rocks, feeling their dampness, how pleasantly they cooled his stomach and chest. He spat dusty, viscous saliva and wondered: Well, can we drink from our canteens now or not? He glanced around, gingerly loosened his belt, raised the canteen to his chest without taking it off the belt, removed the stopper, bent his head, extended his lips to the neck of the canteen, and sucked in a mouthful of water. He swirled it around his mouth and swallowed, thinking it was a pity to spit out. He sucked on the canteen once more, then replaced the stopper, tightened his belt, and thought: Maybe a smoke now.

Only one star, Venus, remained in the sky. The road became light, the *kishlak* seemed closer. The road was deserted. Everyone was watching it, Kostomygin included. He was thinking that all of this was senseless: no one would show up, there wouldn't be any shooting, the sun would simply rise and they would return to camp. It was his first operation, and he didn't believe it would turn out like the ones the company veterans told such vivid stories about.

He grew bored staring at the road along which no one would come, yawned, and closed his eyes to rest them for a while. He fell asleep for no more than a few minutes and awoke with a start. No weakness, he told himself, and once more began to watch the road assiduously.

It became lighter; nightingales began to chirp in the *kishlak*'s gardens and a cock crowed several times in succession, drowning out their trilling with its guttural racket.

When the sky and the steppe began to turn red in the east, a harsh, incantatory wail arose from the *kishlak*. Kostomygin's sleepiness vanished in an instant; he reached for his rifle and, stretching his neck, peered over the rocks. The wail arose again, and Kostomygin's heart sank: This is it, battle. But the soldiers lying near him remained calm. He glanced around at them, deflated, but decided all the same to ask the sparrow Medvedev what was going on. Medvedev grunted and told him in a whisper that it was just the keening of one of their priests.

The sun came up. The steppe extended, greenish, to the horizon, and in the *kishlak* cocks were shrieking, cows lowing, and a donkey braying. The sky was turning a full, radiant blue. To hell with this war, Kostomygin thought.

The captain reappeared, shook himself off, and said, 'You can smoke.'

The soldiers roused themselves, yawned broadly, began to talk to one another, struck matches, inhaled cigarette smoke, shielded their eyes with their hands.

The captain was gloomily watching the *kishlak*.

'Sanych,' he said to the radio operator, 'pull the men back

from the *kishlak* and tell the drivers to get their wagons here now.'

'Comrade captain,' said Shvarev, 'maybe the caravan has passed through already?'

The captain shook his head.

'No. The estimate was that it would take them all night to get here from the mountains. They couldn't have set out before nightfall. So they left late in the evening yesterday and should have reached here early this morning.'

'Unless what?'

'Well, unless they had rocket-powered camels,' the captain answered grudgingly.

The radio operator contacted the platoons in their positions around the *kishlak*, then the BMP drivers and mechanics.

The captain sat down on a rock, took off his cap, pulled out a comb, and unhurriedly began to run it through his hair. Shvarev hovered around him, kicking at pebbles and now and then whistling wistfully.

'What's the matter with you, Shvarev?' the captain asked at last.

'Comrade captain, maybe they managed to slip into the *kishlak* somehow?'

'So our boys were there all night for nothing? Unless, of course, they got some sleep out of it.'

'Maybe, comrade captain, we could just go in and shake the place down a little. Maybe it's packed with guns and *doukhs*.'

The captain thoughtfully blew the comb clear, then deftly slipped it into its sheath and put it away. Shvarev looked at him expectantly.

'How many notches have you got, Shvarev?' the captain asked wearily.

'What notches?'

'On the butt of your gun, Shvarev, the butt of your gun. You think I don't know where you put them? I know everything, Shvarev, and one of these days I'll put you on a charge for malicious destruction of weapons.'

'Oh, it's not destruction – we do it very lightly. A little scratch, that's all,' said the grey-eyed, well built Salikhov with a smile.

'And why do you put notches on the butt of your gun?'

Salikhov reddened and shrugged his shoulders. 'Where else would we put them?'

'You? On your boots and on your fists.'

Everyone burst out laughing.

Everybody else's face is brown, but his is the colour of milk, thought Kostomygin all of a sudden, looking at Salikhov's long, delicate features. Does he have a special dispensation from the sun?

Salikhov was the most popular man in the company. He had a good singing voice and played the guitar beautifully. He never swore at anyone, never bullied the kids, never even shouted at them. He spent all his free time on the playing fields with friends from home who were serving in an infantry company; even their training sessions would attract spectators. If the weather was bad he would lie in bed with a book. In his village back home a wide-eyed, raven-haired girl with a face as milk-white as his was waiting for him; a large photograph of her rested on his bedside locker, and the woman-hungry men in the company would sometimes pick it up and stare at it with voluptuous longing. Salikhov's girlfriend often sent him thick, fat envelopes, and everyone envied him. Around his neck hung a leather pendant with a lock of her hair in it – and everyone envied Salikhov.

Kostomygin wanted to become friends with him. Kostomygin poured his heart out in letters to his brother, but what use was a letter? Real conversation with an intelligent person was something else entirely. He thought that Salikhov was probably anxious for a kindred spirit, but Kostomygin was too shy to go up to him and start talking about serious books and things like that. He wished Salikhov would somehow start up a conversation with him, but Salikhov didn't talk to kids – in fact he hardly seemed to notice them at all.

'So how many scratches have you got on the butt of your gun, Shvarev?' the captain asked. He was watching the platoons return from the *kishlak*.

'Six.'

'Isn't that enough for you?'

'No.'

'You're a real Dracula, Shvarev.'

Everyone laughed.

'What are you cackling for?' the captain asked with a smile. 'Any of you know who Dracula was?'

'No,' someone answered.

'So what the hell are you laughing for?'

'Who was Dracula, comrade captain?' asked the sparrow Medvedev obsequiously. 'Did he put notches on his gun too?'

'No,' the captain answered, 'he was a ruler in the fifteenth century who used to nail helmets.'

'Into heads?' Medvedev ventured. The captain nodded, and everyone laughed as though it were the funniest thing in the world.

'Well, I haven't gone that far yet,' said Shvarev with a contented grin, 'so I couldn't be Dracula.'

'Yes,' the captain agreed. 'There's a difference. He wasn't a sergeant. He was a prince.'

*

The BMPs arrived. The soldiers split up into sections, got out their dry rations – tinned pork, tinned cheese, sugar, bread – and, squatting on the ground between the machines, settled in to breakfast.

Shvarev polished off his can of meat in a flash, rolling his eyes with pleasure, then ate his soft yellow cheese, gulped down all his sugar, drained half his canteen, then paused as though listening for something before sighing: 'That barely made a dent.'

'Yeah,' said Mamedov, one of the drivers, 'and you've g-got such a b-big dent!' He pointed his finger at Shvarev's lean stomach and began to laugh. 'You shovel it all in and don't get any f-fatter. No g-girl will ever fall for you. They only like f-fat men.'

'Well,' Shvarev said, squaring his shoulders, 'well, Mamed, where you come from the ladies may be happy with stomachs, but *our* women – they need something more substantial.' He glanced over at Oparin and shouted, 'What the hell are you grinning at? Get it down. In the field you do everything fast, you eat, you . . .'

Oparin stopped grinning, stuck his spoon into the pinkish meat, and said, 'Comrade sergeant, do you want it? I'd rather just have the cheese.'

Kostomygin looked at Oparin, then turned his head away.

What a creep that Oparin was. He did his best to get along with the old-timers, hoping that they'd take a liking to him and stop kicking his arse all the time. He was the only kid who washed their clothes and leggings for them. The others had flatly refused and had taken a beating for it, but after that no one bothered them. Oparin still did the washing for all the old-timers.

'Whoever buckles in buckles under,' his older brother had

warned him, and after a short time in uniform Kostomygin had come to see that it was true, although now he would add to what his brother had said. But you must always keep a sense of proportion. Krylov, for instance, hadn't learned that; he would refuse to do anything for the old-timers, even the pettiest and least objectionable chore, and in return they made him live 'by the rules'. No one in the army lives by the rules: obeying every regulation day and night would be too much for anyone, any common soldier, any general, any marshal – a single day of living by the rules would leave even the keenest bullshit-artist in tears. So Krylov hadn't been able to take it, and he'd written a gloomy letter home telling the whole story. His relatives had forwarded the letter to the Ministry of Defence, and soon afterwards a commission turned up at camp to conduct an inquiry. Krylov had urged the other kids to tell the truth, but nobody had really wanted to. The kids reckoned, pragmatically enough, that the commission wouldn't sling every last old-timer into a disciplinary battalion, that maybe a couple would be punished but the rest of them would still be around – so Krylov had found himself utterly alone. Over the course of the proceedings it had become clear that Krylov had been treated fairly, or at least by the rules. The matter had been closed and Krylov had been assigned to an auxiliary unit: in the pigsties. Kostomygin often saw him tooling around among the mess tents, covered with dirt, unshaven, carrying pails of slop that he would have to pour out, splashing the swill all over his hands and boots, into a steel barrel mounted on a cart – they called it the 'cabriolet' – that was pulled along by a captured white donkey named Doukh.

No, you had to keep a sense of proportion. Krylov didn't and neither did Oparin – even if he really didn't want the meat he should have offered it to someone of his own rank, to Kostomygin himself, for example. So there were the two poles,

Oparin and Krylov, that you had to avoid. Should I write to my brother, see what he thinks? Kostomygin thought to himself.

'Listen!' Shvarev said sharply. 'If it was winter, and I was really cold, would you give me your coat too? You know what the winters are like here? Brrr!'

'Yeah, b-but by this winter you'll be stuffing yourself on your mama's b-blinis,' Mamedov reminded him.

Shvarev brushed him off. 'Shut it, Mamed. Well, Oparin, would you?'

Oparin cast him a cowed glance.

'Answer me.'

'If it was absolutely necessary . . .' Oparin mumbled, then fell silent.

'And if your girlfriend was here, you'd let me have her too?'

'You're joking, comrade sergeant,' Oparin said, smiling shyly.

'Let's just suppose. Answer me.'

Oparin was flustered, and his eye twitched.

'Answer, you little slob,' hissed Mamedov, his eyes gleaming.

Oparin flinched and said in a barely audible voice, 'It's too . . .'

'What?' yelled Shvarev.

Oparin finished the sentence: 'To suppose that, it's too much.'

'You're a shit, a maggot! How did you manage to get into recon? You should be drummed out, like Krylov. Eat your own damn meat. I don't want it. On an operation you force it down if that's what it takes.'

'Bolt it, and beat 'em,' Mamedov quoted.

'That clear?' said Shvarev. 'Your second mistake so far. You remember the first?'

'Yes,' Oparin answered limply, digging into the meat.

Shvarev lit a cigarette and distractedly looked over at Kostomygin.

'Hey, Kosty, what are you turning your back for? Proud, are you?'

'I'm just watching the *kishlak*,' Kostomygin replied.

'No,' said Mamedov, 'it's not just that. He h-hates Oparin.'

'Do you hate Oparin?' Shvarev asked.

'No,' Kostomygin lied.

'Just watch it. Any second and you'll be in the same boat as him.'

'I think the k-kids are getting a b-bit uppity,' Mamedov noted. He took a swig from his canteen. 'Just yesterday I asked for a civvy cigarette and K-Kosty wouldn't bring me one.'

'Seriously?' Shvarev narrowed his eyes and looked at Kostomygin.

'Yes, we have to k-keep a close eye on the lot of 'em. We k-kick the shit out of Opie but we forget the rest.'

'Fine,' said Shvarev. 'When we get back to camp, Kosty, Mamedov and I want to see a pack of Javas. Opie here will count to a hundred and we'll see a pack of Javas. Got it?'

'Yes,' answered Kostomygin.

'What?'

Kostomygin corrected himself. 'Understood.'

Mamedov shook his head. 'Told you, they're g-getting uppity.'

After breakfast everyone climbed aboard the machines and the column set off for home.

Outside the *kishlak*, on the bank of the river that had shimmered so prettily the night before, the column overtook an ancient open truck, a yellow Toyota filled with armed men in multicoloured turbans and baggy clothes. Next to the driver sat a thin, moustachioed man wearing the uniform of a militia officer. He got out of the truck and, smiling, made his way over to the captain's BMP.

He greeted the captian. *'Mondana bashi khub vesti!'*

The captain climbed down from his machine and shook the man's tawny hand. 'How are things, Akhbar?'

'Khub, commander,' answered the militia officer, his eyes searching for someone among the soldiers on the BMPs. He spotted Kuchechkarov, a Tadzhikistani, and waved to him. 'Akhat!'

The small, dark-haired soldier came down to join them. After clasping the Afghan officer's hand and kissing him three times on his stubbled cheeks, Akhat began to translate. It turned out that the men were on their way to the camp with news that a large caravan laden with arms had made it into Padzhak, a nearby *kishlak*. Unconvinced, the captain asked how they were so sure that the caravan was carrying arms: maybe it was just loaded with cloth or food or something, maybe it was just an ordinary caravan of itinerant traders. The militia officer was offended and insisted that he had people in Padzhak, people with sharp eyes and honest tongues. The captain asked him when the caravan had appeared. At dawn, the officer said. Well then, they've probably left already, the captain suggested, while you were on your way to tell us they simply left again. They wouldn't have left in daylight unless a rabid jackal had bitten them, the officer Akhbar retorted.

'Who are these people?' Kostomygin asked Shvarev.

'Oh, they're from Spinda-Ulya. There's a militia detachment stationed there,' Shvarev said casually. 'The least little thing and they come running to us for help. But they're great hosts. Mamed, you remember their shashlik?'

Mamedov nodded and clicked his tongue in delight.

'Well, looks as if something's up,' said Shvarev, his eyes sparkling. 'Hey, Kosty, Opie! It'll be your baptism! I have a feeling they weren't headed to the camp for nothing.'

The moustache was losing patience, gesticulating angrily, trying to convince the captain that his information was true. The captain was already beginning to suspect that it probably was – the caravan they had been waiting for had veered off into Padzhak, and that was that – but nevertheless he continued to question Akhbar about every little detail: how many camels, how many men, had anyone out of the ordinary shown up recently, and so on. Only after all that did he radio back to camp and try to get in touch with the unit CP. The CP answered about ten minutes later.

After talking to the CP, the captain waved to Akhbar, swung his machine around, and headed off down the road that led back along the river. The whole column followed, the Afghans in their battered Toyota bringing up the rear.

'It'll be your baptism, my sons!' shouted Shvarev, slapping Kostomygin on the back. Oparin's face assumed an expression of joy, and he began to punch the air with his assault rifle.

The column was flying along the sparkling little river amid swirling clouds of sunlit dust. The column was roaring, spewing palls of black exhaust, crunching gravel loudly under its tracks, and Kostomygin, hypnotized by the deafening noise and the speed of their movement through the sunlight, the dust, and the rich absinthe smell of the steppes, was thinking that he would write his brother a letter, a really crazy letter. That night, that aroma of flowery gardens, that moon, these hills under the stars, the nightingales, the ambush they'd laid, the muezzin's howling at dawn, their disappointment, and then this meeting, the sun, the dust, the clattering, the soot, and now expectation, uncertainty. What would happen in Padzhak? What would Padzhak look like? How would they take the caravan? How many rebels would they find? What would they look like – savage, bearded? Who would die – didn't someone have to die? If Oparin, for instance, was killed . . . He was sitting here now, and in an hour he'd be dead. Or even Kostomygin himself – he'd have time for his whole life to flash before his eyes, then he'd die in the dust, scorched by the sun, they'd send his body home, his family and friends would cry and cry . . .

But he was sure that this time it would all be real, he'd write to his brother about his first real operation, and he would write to him because he wouldn't die, in fact he would never die – well, of course, some time he probably would, but the devil only knew when, years and years from now, a century.

Padzhak turned out to be a smallish *kishlak* not much different from any of the ones Kostomygin had seen already: grey *duval*s, some high, some low, grey towers, some round, some polygonal, grey houses, square or rectangular, all of them looking like narrow-windowed little boxes, and very rich, very lush gardens. Padzhak stood on a riverbank. The steppes that surrounded it were already brown and sparse, but the gardens of Padzhak were green and flourishing. The column had barely reached the *kishlak* when Kostomygin smelled its fragrant aroma, and once again that sweetness was in his mouth.

For fear of snipers the soldiers slipped on their helmets and flak jackets and took cover behind the machines. But the *kishlak* seemed utterly peaceful: roosters were strutting along the *duval*s, an old man was leading a humpbacked cow down a street, and inquisitive children were scampering around, sticking their necks out for a peek at the *kafir*s and their dust-covered machines.

'Yes, we've got our little doves now,' said Shvarev, drawing on a cigarette.

'What are we waiting for?' asked Kostomygin.

'Impatient, eh?' Shvarev smiled. 'Uncle Vitya knows what he's doing.' ('Uncle Vitya' was what the old-timers called the captain among themselves.) 'Don't worry, he knows his stuff.' But half an hour later even Shvarev was beginning to fidget and cast puzzled glances towards the captain's machine.

'Mamed,' he called out to the BMP driver, 'why do you think he's dragging his feet?'

Mamedov shrugged. 'God knows. Maybe the CP is s-sending us some infantry.'

Shvarev frowned. 'How many can there be in that caravan, anyway? Ten, maybe, what, twenty at the outside?'

'B-but what if the whole *kishlak* rises up?'

'If we wait for infantry the *doukh*s will bury all the guns and we'll never be able to prove it's the same caravan we've been waiting for all night.' Shvarev spat into the dust.

'No, it's b-better to wait,' countered Mamedov. 'More fun with the infantry here t-too.'

'Comrade sergeant, can I have a drink now?' Oparin asked.

'You "can" go and taking a flying fuck,' Shvarev yelled back.

Oparin corrected himself. 'Permission to drink?'

'On an operation you have to conserve water,' Shvarev answered.

Oparin sighed and stole a glance at the shimmering river.

'What are you looking at the river for? Only donkeys and natives drink river water, and the slime doesn't affect them. Im-mu-ni-ty. You'd get yellow fever that way. Or typhus. Or some sort of syphilis.'

'Got it,' said Oparin, and he ran his dry tongue over the black crust that fringed his lips.

Shvarev heard something and froze.

'What is it?' Mamedov asked.

'Looks as though they're here.'

Then they all heard the distant rumble, turned their heads, and began to scan the road. Soon they could make out clouds of dust on the steppe.

Kostomygin groped for the safety catch on his assault rifle and flicked it to full automatic.

An infantry company and four tanks were heading towards the *kishlak*. Less than ten minutes later the operation began.

Akhat Kuchechkarov raised the megaphone to his face and shouted a few short phrases into the *kishlak*, then paused for a few moments and shouted again.

Telling them to surrender, Kostomygin thought.

A few minutes passed, but no one appeared or came out. Kostomygin stared at the *kishlak*, astonished, unable to understand how its inhabitants had managed to clear the streets of all the chickens and donkeys and children. The place was deserted and silent.

Akhat looked over inquiringly to the captain. The captain said, 'That's enough.' Akhat dropped the megaphone into the hatch.

A few BTRs and BMPs slowly advanced into the *kishlak*, followed by helmeted and flak-jacketed soldiers with their rifles at the ready. They entered from one direction only – to avoid shooting one another, Kostomygin supposed – and fanned out into the alleys.

The *kishlak* was silent.

Someone pounded on a door with the butt of his gun. Kostomygin flinched when he heard the harsh sound of the blows against wood.

'Over here,' Shvarev said, swinging towards a house that was entirely surrouned by a low *duval*. He kicked the heavy gate. It opened a few moments later and out into the street came a bony old man, leaning on a cane. He had a wrinkled face, yellowish hands covered by translucent skin, and a look of indifference in his eyes.

'*Nis, nis dushman*,' he croaked.

Shvarev swept past him, saying nothing, and went into the courtyard.

'Medved! The gateway!' he shouted, then ran into the house. Oparin, Kostomygin, Salikhov, and a few men from the infantry company rushed in after him.

They searched the whole two-storey building but found no one except a little group of children and women in chadors crowded into a small room in the remotest part of the house, found nothing but rags, crockery, and food.

One of the infantrymen suggested stripping the chadors off – who knew if they really were women? But Salikhov rejected the idea out of hand, and since everyone in the regiment knew who he was and at one time or another had seen what he was capable of on the playing field, even among friends, no one dared to overrule him now.

They went out into the courtyard.

'We'll check the barn,' Shvarev said. They were just about to do so when there was a crackle of gunfire and the wooden gates creaked. The soldiers hurried to the entryway.

Medvedev was leaning against the gate, gasping loudly for breath.

Gunfire erupted all over the *kishlak*. The soldiers started shooting back through windows and at the gardens and rooftops. A machine-gun was hammering and a grenade exploded.

One of the BMPs lumbered up, and they dragged Medvedev towards the machine. Kostomygin stared dumbly while they hauled the wounded man aboard and dropped him into the hatch. Through his legs he felt a sort of trembling in the earth, and he looked down. He was flabbergasted by what he saw.

Little plumes of dust were rising up from the ground at his feet. He hurled himself backwards against the *duval*.

'Over here!' bellowed Shvarev. Kostomygin came back to his senses and ran into the entryway. Splinters were flying off the wooden gate and he threw his hands up to protect his face.

'What is it, what is it?' Shvarev yelled, pulling Kostomygin's hands apart. 'What is it?' Shvarev bent down to examine him. 'Ah! Nothing! Splinters!'

Kostomygin rubbed his eyes, blinked a few times, and looked around.

'What should I do?' he asked Shvarev.

'Shoot at that house!' Shvarev pointed at the house next door, then fired a volley into one of its windows.

And Kostomygin, taking cover behind the *duval*, began to unleash long bursts of fire into the building.

'Shithead!' yelled Shvarev. 'Don't waste ammo!'

It was hot, dust was gritting in his teeth, and more than anything he wanted to take off this hot, heavy helmet and this cumbersome flak jacket. Kostomygin would fire off a short burst, pause for a moment, then pop up again from behind the *duval* and rattle off a few rounds through a window into the tall, vast house, but he couldn't manage to hit the machine-gunner, who fired from one window, ducked, then moved to another and fired from there.

Gunfire was raging all over the *kishlak*. Now and then a grenade exploded. There was dust in the air and a strong smell of gunpowder.

The rapid-fire cannons of the BMPs were roaring, machine-guns firing, loud and heavy. The stench of powder mixed with the scent of trees in blossom made Kostomygin feel sick. He was becoming desperately tired of raising himself halfway up, shooting, crouching down again, then getting back up, pulling the trigger, and yet again ducking back down behind the *duval*. It was so hot, the powder and the flowers were reeking so much, Kostomygin's ears were ringing, his throat was parched, the machine-gunner kept hammering and hammering, and none of this would ever end, Medvedev was no doubt whimpering, in agony, in the stifling interior of the BMP, none of it would ever end . . . Which window would the machine-gunner fire from next? And where was Oparin?

Kostomygin turned his head and to his left saw a damp red face with bulging eyes. His feeling of nausea grew worse. He wanted to force Oparin to shoot, not just to keep standing there next to the *duval*, paralysed, head bowed, assault rifle hanging limply from his arms, but all of a sudden he realized that the machine-gunner wasn't firing any more. He cautiously peered out and stole a glance at the dark empty windows. He stuck his head out further and saw that coming from the house into the courtyard was a broad-shouldered man with his hands in the air. Behind him was a young boy, hunched over, and then, behind them both, Salikhov and one of the infantrymen.

'They got them!' Kostomygin cried out, shocked, to Shvarev.

Shvarev, already on the run, called out, 'Opie! Kosty!' Kostomygin and Oparin ran after him.

They ran into the street, reached the gates of the neighbouring house, and entered through a narrow little door.

Without saying a word Shvarev ran up to the lean, broad-shouldered, hook-nosed man dressed in a long tattered blue shirt, and struck him in the chin with the butt of his gun. The hook-nosed man's head jerked back, but he stayed on his feet. The wide-eyed boy standing just behind him reeled and cried out as if it were he who had just been hit. The man straightened up. Blood was streaming from his mouth.

'Which one of these shits got Medvedev?' Shvarev yelled.

Baptism

The man looked at him sullenly, his jaw muscles flexing under the black stubble that covered his cheeks. The boy pulled the grubby turban off his head and buried his face in it.

'Now what?' asked Salikhov.

'They shot Medvedev,' Shvarev said, looking round.

Salikhov nodded.

'Right.' Shvarev wiped the sweat off his face with his sleeve. 'That's it. *Murd*, lads, *murd*. That's it, *khana*,' he said to the prisoners. The boy's shoulders began to tremble, and the man's eyes narrowed.

'So,' Shvarev muttered. 'Right . . .' He looked around again, his eyes met Oparin's, and he said again, 'Right.'

'Then let's do it quickly,' the infantryman said in a low voice, 'before an officer sees them.' He moved closer to the boy and raised the barrel of his rifle to the turban that was still shrouding his face.

Shvarev stopped him. 'Hold it.' He looked around once more, then glanced at Kostomygin and Oparin. 'Wait. Kosty! You take the man. Opie! You finish off the other one.'

'Let the youngsters do it? Sure, why not?' the infantryman said approvingly, then stepped aside.

Kostomygin felt as though the back of his neck had turned to ice. It was horrifying, in this heat, for anything to feel so cold. His teeth began to chatter. He clamped down on them and looked at Shvarev. What was he saying, and to whom?

'Now!' Shvarev yelled.

The sun hung low over the steppe; the steppe beneath it and the swathe of sky above it were glowing crimson, and the bitter, scorching air was slowly cooling off.

The long column was snaking its way over the twilit steppe, banners of grey dust fluttering over it. The column was heading back to camp. The soldiers, shoulders slumped with exhaustion, were sitting on top of their machines. The prisoners rode inside, hands bound.

Dust was caking their eyes and catching in their throats, but the soldiers would not ride in the interior of the BMPs; anyone inside would be mashed against its metal walls if one of the machines hit a mine, but if you were sitting on top you'd just be thrown to the ground. It was a simple truth known to everyone who fought in Afghanistan. The prisoners taken with the caravan knew it too; they would sweat and quiver whenever the machine they were in ran over a pothole or hit a boulder with its undercarriage, and pray to Allah that He remove all mines from their path. Or maybe they were praying for Him to send everyone – the detested *kafirs* and they themselves – to hell with one mighty explosion. The truth was, if a BMP ran over a mine very few would live to tell the tale: the ten-ton machine would flip onto its back like an empty tin can, and anyone sitting on top would be flattened into a pancake.

The column was bringing back to camp eleven prisoners and a mass of war trophies: Italian-made land mines, large-calibre machine-guns, grenade-launchers, crates of ammunition and grenades, and a whole shipment of American and West German medical supplies.

The infantry officers were pleased with the operation and knew that the CP would be pleased too. The commander of the reconnaissance company was gloomy and sour: Medvedev had died on the road home – the bullet had torn through his intestines – and the leader of the first platoon, a lieutenant, had a serious head wound. They hadn't managed to do a clean job this time.

Kostomygin, the only man in the whole unit to ride inside a BMP, was lying back on a crate of shells. He was chain-smoking and didn't give a damn if the machine ran over a mine or not. All the same to me, he thought angrily.

It was true: whether or not the machine blew up made absolutely no difference to him. He was thinking about Oparin and Salikhov and the hook-nosed man with the bloodstained lips. He wanted not to think about any of it, he just wanted to fall asleep, to sleep any way he could, to sleep such a sleep that he wouldn't wake up for a thousand years, nor remember anything afterwards. But it was impossible not to think, not to remember. He thought, he remembered.

He remembered everything precisely, even though during the battle itself he had felt as though he was someone else, and the events had been ghostly and confused. But now everything was crystal-clear, like a film in slow motion.

He remembered it all vividly, every sound, every noise, every movement. He remembered how the ground under his feet had trembled, how the wooden gates had splintered and slivers of wood had flown into his face, how they had run through the dimly lit rooms in that house, how one of the infantrymen had suggested checking the women under those veils to see if they had moustaches. And he remembered how he had grown tired of firing into the windows of the house next door, and then he saw the hook-nosed man coming out into the courtyard, his hands in the air, and then the boy, then Salikhov and the infantryman . . . But still, wasn't it interesting, the way they had pulled the thing off? Interesting, shit – what difference did that make now? He couldn't care less.

He had fired a short burst into the broad chest of the hook-nosed man, and the man had fallen down, twisted in the dirt, blown scarlet bubbles from his nose, then stopped moving.

. . . But Medvedev had died on the way back to camp. Was he really dead? It meant nothing . . .

And Oparin? Who would have believed it? Who the hell would have believed it?

Kostomygin thought about Oparin. He hated Oparin. He remembered how he had turned round and seen that sweaty red face, a coward's face with bulging eyes, and he groaned with hatred and loathing.

He didn't do it, because he's a coward. A coward, a coward, Kostomygin repeated to himself, but it didn't make him feel any better.

Oparin had not fired. Shvarev had threatened him and screamed at him, but Oparin had not fired. What would it have cost him to pull the trigger, what the hell would it have cost him? He had burst into tears and begged them to let him go. Let him go? Where? Home to mama? He had fallen apart completely, bawling his eyes out, begging them to let him go. God, what they'd do to him back at camp!

Why should I care what they do to that shit? To hell with him. He's a coward, he'll always be a coward, he's not even worth thinking about. That Salikhov, though . . .

Kostomygin pulled on a cigarette. He had already smoked himself to the point of nausea, he was barely able to keep himself from being sick, but he reached into the pack for another and lit it from the one before. That Salikhov. Kostomygin wondered, frowning. He hadn't really been there, had he?

But Salikhov had been there, in that narrow little courtyard too. He and the infantryman who'd helped him capture the rebel machine-gunners.

Yes, Salikhov had been there too, and once it had dawned on Salikhov that Oparin wouldn't shoot, that Oparin would rather have shot himself instead, once that had dawned on him, Salikhov had walked up to the boy, who still had his face buried in the dirty, tattered turban, and he had killed him with one

backhand blow. He had killed him barehanded, and no one had
felt any surprise. He did it so quickly that you might have
thought that the boy had just . . . died – that his heart had
stopped all of a sudden and he had just fallen down dead.

Kostomygin, buffeted around on top of the shell-filled crates,
took another drag from his cigarette, and he didn't want to die in
some distant future, in a thousand years. He wanted his heart to
stop right there and then. But it didn't stop.

Unit N Carried Out Exercises

Day and night the battalions had been storming the Iskapol mountains in the province of Gazin. Howitzer and rocket batteries, aircraft, and fast, narrow, speckled helicopters poured tons of steel onto the hills. The cold autumn air smelled of gunpowder, and dust clouded the sun and stars. During the day helicopters came for the dead and wounded. At night, moonless and starry, a transport plane circled high above the hills and dropped flare packs that burst into handfuls of orange suns. The fluttering spheres would slowly sink down, lighting the ravines, cliffs, and heights, as well as the steppe that extended around the hills, where the regiment's field camp lay. The infantry would climb up accompanied by the thudding of heavy machine-guns, explosions, the clatter of rapid-firing grenade launchers. When the orange suns died out the infantry would dive to the ground. After a short lull the artillery officers would shout loudly from the steppe below and the preliminary barrage would begin.

The rebels, firmly entrenched in caves and outcrops of rock, had a large base in these mountains and were well stocked with water, food, medical supplies and ammunition. They were fighting with insulting effectiveness.

When the howitzers and rocket installations fell silent one

could make out, under the stars, the mournful, indistinct drone of the transport plane's engines. The infantrymen lay prone against the rocks, wiping their sweat-damp and dirt-encrusted faces and raising canteens to blistered lips, waiting for the hiss of flares up above.

Silence, darkness.

The men caught their breath, drank their water, and began to feel the cold – it was autumn, and though the sun warmed during the day, at night the air was icy and dried off the soldiers' sweat within moments after an attack.

They waited.

Something was delaying the transport plane; the infantrymen were starting to become used to the quiet.

A few more minutes passed and then there was a hiss and a crackle above them – the flares lighting up. The captain shouted, 'Company, forward!' The men got up and started to climb. A machine-gun hammered overhead and tracer began to skitter against the rocks, bullets ricocheting into the air in every direction. The infantrymen leaped from outcrop to outcrop, firing off short bursts, their faces burning, their stomachs freezing cold. One of the red-hot streams of bullets cut into a soldier running up the hill; he collapsed – it was the captain – and spat blood, then didn't move any more. He was dead. A lieutenant took over and the attack was resumed.

The lieutenant led the company towards the summit, where the rebels had dug themselves in on a crest. The rebels were on the verge of losing the heights; their heavy machine-gun had stopped firing and they were shooting with pistols and assault rifles. Battle was raging everywhere on the summit and shells were exploding on the next hill. The company closed in, lobbed grenades onto the crest, and the assault rifles and pistols fell silent. After a pause, motioning for the others to follow, the lieutenant was the first to fling himself over the top.

Beyond some boulders was a flat little plateau on which the heavy machine-gun stood; scattered around it lay empty metal shell-casings and four bodies torn to pieces by shrapnel. A fifth man was dragging himself downhill. The lieutenant caught him, kicked him, and the rebel rolled over onto his back and raised his shattered hands. After ordering the soldiers to drag him back to the little plateau, the lieutenant radioed the battalion commander a report on the winning of the crest and the casualties they had taken. The commander ordered him to leave a few machine-gunners behind on the captured hill and to strike the neighbouring one from the north. Four men stayed while the rest of the company climbed back down.

The soldiers left behind on the hill drank and smoked.

The wounded man whimpered; his hands were in tatters and he had been shot in the leg. The four bodies, blood still seeping from them, were lying motionless. The machine-gunners, glad to be staying here, inhaled their acrid smoke. Maybe it was all over for the time being and they wouldn't have to go through that hell again: in the morning the whole regiment would head home, laden with war trophies, to its tent city, where there were baths, clean sheets, meals three times a day, letters, films every night, pay-coupons – and, in the canteen, filter-tip cigarettes, marmalade, biscuits, condensed milk, Indian coffee, grapefruit juice. Not to mention Tanya in the library, who never glanced twice at the soldiers though they certainly looked at her; she had red lips, heavyish legs with little tendrils of black hair on them, large, prominent buttocks; she sweated and her shirt was always damp under her arms and along the crook of her back, but you could go to the library any time to look at Tanya and smell her aroma of perfume and sweat. And now the captain would miss all that for ever. Dead? Nothing had ever touched him before, not bullets, not yellow fever, not typhus. Once he and a soldier had been coming down a *kiariz*, flashlights in hand, following an underground corridor. The corridor suddenly made a sharp turn and on the other side they ran into some rebels, so the two opened fire and threw themselves backwards. The first one they pulled out of the *kiariz* was the soldier, who had been shot in the calf. The captain was alive and completely unharmed. And now he was dead.

Cigarettes are great; only idiots give up smoking. Or drinking – teetotallers are fools. After an operation you'd give a year of your life for a bottle of vodka. You wash yourself clean in the baths, then you pour yourself, in your standard-issue cup, some pure, bitter-tasting vodka. They ship it from home in tanker trucks and it costs thirty coupons, expensive but what the hell. You pour yourself some. The amount in your cup is worth roughly seven coupons, nearly the monthly pay of a private. But who cares: for half an hour you feel like a human being, no boredom, no fear, your brain sparkles, and two years – that's nothing.

The shooting died down on the other crest: a lull.

'On your toes, men,' said the sergeant in command of the group.

The machine-gunners were already alert.

Up above the transport plane was droning. Not a bad job, being a pilot. It wasn't the artillerymen who were gods, but them, in their black leather helmets and blue flight suits. But of course they got it, too – the rebels loved going after aircraft, and above all they loved to get their hands on the crews of shot-down planes and helicopters. There wasn't anything worse than being taken prisoner in the East. The rebels knew how to kill slowly, rationing out death by degrees. The company had once found the body of an NCO who'd been through two days of it: a swollen bluish-grey carcass with grey hair that only the captain could identify. Rather anything in the world than be taken prisoner. No, the gods of this war weren't the artillerymen or the pilots but the staff officers. But even they died – although rarely enough – since after all they were in the war too, not above it. The gods were elsewhere, above it.

'The artillery's about to hit them,' one of the machine-gunners said in a hoarse voice. 'If they don't clobber us instead. They're thick enough to do just that.'

'The lieutenant spoke to them on the radio,' the sergeant responded.

The prisoner moaned and everyone glanced at him. He wrapped his hands in the long folds of his shirt but blood began to seep through the cloth.

'They killed the captain,' the sergeant said.

No one answered him.

The captive's broken hands were itching and burning. It felt as if they were being devoured by clouds of hairy insects whose jagged pincers were ripping into his skin, his flesh, into his veins and cartilage, their sheer number and weight pulling his arms downwards. The prisoner lay on the ground, his back against a boulder, and clutched his hands to his chest.

They killed the captain, thought the sergeant. Again he glanced over at the prisoner.

A spasm hit the wounded man.

His hands should be bandaged, thought Grashchenkov, a machine-gunner who had been shot in the thigh in his first few days of service.

Under the stars came the mournful engine sound of the invisible transport plane.

Soon the rocket installations and the 122-millimetre howitzers will open up, everything will burst into flames, start to rock, shudder – soon . . .

In the silence the hoarse-voiced gunner said, 'Something's flying past over there.'

The soldiers scanned the sky and made out a glimmering speck far away, high above the steppe, an aircraft on the horizon. It seemed to be a passenger jet; it was flying from north to south, sailing noiselessly through the sky, navigation lights blinking on its wings and underbelly, making its way towards India or Pakistan. The soldiers watched its pulsing lights.

The lieutenant hunched over, drew a pack of cigarettes from his breast pocket, started smoking. The others, smelling the smoke, lit up too, cupping their cigarettes in their hands. Silence. Was it all over? The rebels had surrendered, the all-clear signal would come soon, and in the morning the battalions would return to camp.

The prisoner whimpered more loudly and they all stared at him. Grashchenkov took his pack off his shoulders, undid it, and pulled out his personal kit. The others thought he'd decided to eat something, and since they were hungry too they unslung their packs, took out their biscuits, tin cans, and sugar, prising the cans open with their bayonets. The smell of sausage meat wafted up. Grashchenkov tore open his packet; bandages and gauze glimmered white in his hands. The sergeant stopped eating and looked at him.

'What are you doing?' he asked.

'I'm going to bandage his wounds.'

'Put those away.'

'Why?'

'We can't waste them,' the sergeant said.

'Speak for yourself. I can waste mine.'

The others were eating their meat, crunching their biscuits, looking around at the darkened hilltops, silently casting glances at the sergeant and the soldier with the bandages.

'You hear what I said, Grashchenkov?' the sergeant asked.

The prisoner was lying back, eyes closed, hearing nothing. Houris in translucent gowns were dancing around him, lifting him by the arms towards the top of a green mountain where, in the shade of the pale rose Lotus, true believers were lying around, chalices in their hands, drinking tea and looking with smiling eyes at the visitor; perfume emanated from the Lotus, fountains with arching streams of iridescent water surrounded it, and above the Lotus white doves flittered back and forth . . .

There was no preliminary artillery barrage; the transport plane dropped flare packs.

'No. I'm going to dress his wounds,' said Grashchenkov. He stood up and headed towards the captive, but a burst of machine-gun fire got there first. Grashchenkov looked at the orange-coloured face, its mouth torn, an eyeball dangling, its nose twisted off to the side.

'A bit more time would have been nice,' the hoarse-voiced soldier commented, stashing the rest of his meat, sugar, and biscuits back into his pack. The second soldier turned aside and quickly polished off his own can, threw it away, licked his spoon clean, popped his lump of sugar into his mouth, and took a swig from his canteen.

Meanwhile the battle on the crest had started up again. While waiting for the green flares, the machine-gunners trained their sights on the neighbouring summit, which the whole company was now stealing up on from the north. The sky was orange, the hills were orange, and the shadows and crags had turned deep black. Muzzle flashes leaped up and down the slope, red streams of gunfire intersected each other, grenades exploded. Their minds blank, the machine-gunners lay on the rocks, which were turning colder and colder, stared at the neighbouring summit, at the intertwining bursts of tracer bullets, and waited.

'The company's got lost,' the hoarse-voiced soldier ventured. 'They've got scattered all to hell.' But just then, as though anxious to prove him wrong, a brilliant flash hit the summit and a bright ball of green light stretched down the side of the hill.

'Fire!' the sergeant ordered furiously.

The machine-gunners opened up on the summit, the company climbing the hill began to shoot, a second company started up from the southern slope, and assault rifles hit the rebels from the west.

'They're in for it now,' the hoarse-voiced soldier said.

But the rebels held their own and bullets began to whizz over the heads of the machine-gunners.

'They're still in for it,' the hoarse-voiced soldier repeated, loosing off long bursts into the neighbouring summit. Suddenly he moaned, stood up, arched his back, his desperate fingers trying to prise a flame out of his spine, then fell.

The sergeant glanced back and saw dark figures in the middle of the slope to their rear. He fired a burst at them and cried out when a sharp invisible claw ripped his shoulder open. Grashchenkov and the second soldier turned around and, balancing the machine-gun in his arms, Grashchenkov began to spray the slope with bullets.

'Behind the rocks!' the sergeant shouted, throwing himself over a boulder. The second soldier leaped over and hurled himself to the ground.

'Grashchenkov!' shouted the sergeant.

Grashchenkov stepped backwards, dropped the machine-gun, raised his hands to his chest, slumped down into a squat, and began to cough wetly. The second machine-gunner crawled towards him, grabbed him by his flak jacket, pulled him down, and dragged him behind a boulder. He took out his first-aid kit, tore it open, and reached for the bandages and gauze. Grashchenkov was lying on his back, not saying anything, wiping his bloody lips over and over again. He looked at the orange sky, not saying anything. He felt no pain. He felt clouded and languid, as though he'd just drunk a whole bottle of vodka by himself. Bullets were skittering off the rocks. The soldier applied a wad of gauze to his lips and the little white cushion immediately filled up and darkened. The soldier quickly removed Grashchenkov's flak jacket and fatigues. Grashchenkov groaned and coughed, beginning to feel the pain at last, and the dark wad of gauze fell from his lips. The soldier picked it up again and wiped his cheeks and chin with it.

'Christ, get some dressings on him,' the sergeant said, but the soldier just kept wiping away the blood Grashchenkov spat up each time he coughed.

'You keep shooting, I'll take over!' the sergeant shouted, crawling to Grashchenkov and pushing the stupefied soldier aside. The soldier picked up the machine-gun and pulled the trigger. The sergeant took out his kit, pulled bandages and gauze from it, found the wounds gurgling on Grashchenkov's chest, and, wincing from the pain in his shoulder, began to bandage him. He finally managed to do it, more or less, but Grashchenkov stopped twitching, his limbs stretched out, and he quickly grew stiff.

'That's it,' the sergeant said, gingerly touching his own hot, wet shoulder.

'We have to get out before we're surrounded!' the soldier shouted, dropping the machine-gun and picking up his assault rifle. 'The magazines are all empty!'

'Grashchenkov's got more!'

But Grashchenkov's pack was resting on the section of the crest where most of the gunfire was crackling.

'Let's get out of here! Back down the hill!' shouted the soldier, crawling back to the rear. Wheezing with pain, the sergeant followed him.

They reached the middle of the slope, stood up and broke into a crouched run, but red tracer ricocheted all around them and they dropped back down. The shooting came from everywhere: above, below, from the path they were trying to retreat along. The sergeant and the soldier began to return fire.

Moments later the sergeant's gun misfired and fell silent, quickly followed by the soldier's.

'What now, Jenya?'

The sergeant said nothing.

'Jenya, you alive?' the soldier called out.

'Grenades . . . You got any?' the sergeant asked.

'No.'

'Then here.'

'What's this for?'

'Take it.' The sergeant dropped a grenade into the soldier's hand and pulled the pin from another. He pressed the pale metal plate of the detonator to the grenade's ribbed body with his fist, then thrust his hand under his body.

'What are . . . No, wait,' the soldier said, crawling off in the other direction. 'You don't have to – '

The sergeant lay on his stomach and didn't say anything. Up above them figures appeared in silhouette – men were creeping stealthily down the slope. The detonator clicked, there was a hollow-sounding explosion; the sergeant rocked, then was thrown up and onto his side. The rebels opened fire. The last machine-gunner threw his grenade to the ground, tore his handkerchief from his pocket, waved it over his head, and yelled: '*Doust!* I give up! No, don't shoot! *Mondana boshchi . . . khub vesti!*'

Mars and the Soldier

1

The room was bright – there had been a snowfall in the night. The first snow had always elated and invigorated him, but today the old man was not well. He had woken up, seen Moscow covered in white, and it had suddenly struck him that this first snow would be his last. The old man drove away the thought, the dark thought of white snow, tried to think of other things instead, and he did, but something inside him pined, aching and burning with grief. And then the pains in his old body faded away; his heart began to beat evenly, his head became clear, but his mood remained sombre. The old man yawned sadly and furrowed his thick black brows.

After breakfast, dressed in a dark blue woollen two-piece suit, the old man sat in his armchair, laid his fleshy white hands on his large soft belly, and through watery eyes looked at Moscow, his vast white Moscow . . .

2

Sorokoputov warmed up a little by rolling around in the narrow, narrow cave; he contorted himself, pulled his knees into his chest, and remained like that, rigid. His arms, tied behind his back with rope, felt heavy and half-dead. From time to time he wriggled his fingers, but his blood was flowing too slowly through the constricted veins anyway and his hands were freezing, growing more and more numb. Sorokoputov didn't know how long he had been in this rocky crevice – maybe a day, maybe a day and a night. He needed water and cigarettes.

It was cold. Sorokoputov was lying on his side, rolled up in a ball, listening to the muffled sounds of battle that had started up again a short time before. Shells were landing dully in the surrounding mountains. That inspired hope. No – hope had never abandoned him, not for an instant. From the very first he had known that all of this was nonsense and foolishness, that in a few moments he would hear shouts, cheering; the heavy slab of stone would move aside and deft, helpful hands would pull him out of this crypt, cut the rope, raise a lighted match to his cigarette. 'Hey, Sorokoputov, how the hell did you get through?' 'God only knows, somehow it just happened. Like in a dream.' 'Sure, Sorokoputov, now you'll have something to tell the ladies.'

He knew that everything would end up precisely that way. It was a feeling, a feeling of good fortune that nothing could undermine. Everything would be all right; all he had to do was be patient and wait.

Sorokoputov lay on the stones, listening for explosions, waiting.

3

How does the poet have it? 'Here the snow like cherry blossoms, here cherry trees blooming as though covered with snow . . .' thought the old man in the blue two-piece suit. He was looking out of his large window at the snowbound city. Soon it will be spring . . . If I live till then. He picked up a slender volume, his favourite. In moments of sorrow he loved to read these poems, even though they made him sadder still. A fleeting idea: 'Their mouths would all be agape.' He imagined them all, mouths gaping, staring with round sheeplike eyes at the slender volume of poems in their sovereign's hands. Him and that poet – rake, scandalmonger, womanizer, suicide. Yes! I love! . . . , the old man said to them all in his mind, then smiled bitterly. He put on his gold-rimmed spectacles, opened the little book, and slowly leafed through a few pages until he found something about snow and a cherry tree: 'The cherry tree is shedding snow . . .'

4

Everything would be all right. The most important thing was not to lose that presentiment of good fortune. Most important . . . yes, most . . . What is the most important thing? Well, it's . . .

Sorokoputov was hanging from a branch over a distant rushing river. His arms were tied and he was gripping the branch in his teeth. They were being torn out of his gums with a cracking sound; he couldn't spit them out, so he would have to swallow them. Soon he would fall, crash into the river, die. He fell headlong towards the water but landed smoothly; he strained his arms, the rope broke, and then he was swimming. The sun was shining, the water was warm, and the riverbanks were covered with large red flowers on a background of green. Some sort of clumsy birds were flying low over the water, gentle, downy birds with feminine eyes that grazed him with their wings. He was laughing . . .

Sorokoputov woke up thinking that he had once had the same dream before. Or no, it had actually happened. Yes, it had – he and a friend had been fishing in the Dnieper at the end of May; it was hot, they had gone swimming, and in the sky gulls were fluttering, storks and herons soaring. After swimming they had lain down on a sandbar, a hot and yellow sandbar. They had sat next to it in the evening, listening to pike splashing in the water. It had rained during the night, and in the morning wild roses had blossomed all around their tent.

The sounds of battle approached. Somewhere nearby, very close, grenades were exploding and a large-calibre machine-gun was pounding relentlessly.

What was it? Day, night?

Voices, they're cheering! Mow the *doukh*s down with machine-guns and get me out of here – well, where are you, you cowards?

Sorokoputov waited.

The most important thing was not to lose faith. In time anyone who doesn't believe in his own fate is killed. But he believes – he knows that sunlight will soon scatter into the cave. The ones who don't make it are the ones who don't really believe, the ones who don't understand life or know what happiness is. But he understands, he knows – it's rain at night and the blossoming of wild roses in the morning.

Sorokoputov flinched when he heard a grinding of stone. The slab was moved aside and a harsh light, like the rays of dozens of projectors, burst into the cave. The noise of explosions and machine-gun fire poured in, and Sorokoputov was deafened, blinded. Hands grabbed his legs and he was dragged out of the stone crevice.

He squinted, saw nothing, then made out the bright sun and white mountaintops. Standing over him were men in long, flowing shirts, fur-lined waistcoats, woollen cloaks, turbans, and astrakhan caps. The light brought tears to his eyes and the drops trickled down his dirt-encrusted cheeks. Over the heads of the men with dark, thin faces hung mountaintops covered with the year's first snow. The gelid air was shaking with explosions and machine-gun bursts.

One of the rebels, a broad-shouldered man with a grey beard, made a sign with his hand: get up. Sorokoputov rose quickly to his feet. He stood on his cramped, trembling legs, his teeth chattering, and looked into the greybeard's eyes. They were exhausted, dark, moist. Sorokoputov looked into them with hope.

The greybeard nodded his head and machine-guns opened up from the left and the right. A searing wind struck Sorokoputov in the chest; he fell on his back, turned over onto his side, hunched himself up. Sorokoputov's legs twisted in the new-fallen snow, and he moaned, breathing scarlet bubbles from his nose.

5

The old man was reading poems in his armchair by the window. He read about a bitch and her pups, about a cow and her calves, about the leaves falling from a maple tree, about an *izba* with blue shutters, about vanished youth, cherry trees and apple trees in bloom. He sighed and moved his black, youthful-looking brows.

The old man turned to another page with his thick white fingers. He buried himself in a new poem and his heavy, porous face began to quiver:

> We are dying,
> We leave in grief and silence
> But I know
> That . . .

The old man tightened his lips and frowned. He read on:

> But I know
> That Russia won't forget us.

The old man's protruding lower lip started to tremble, then his lower jaw, then his head, and a heavy salted tear rolled down the page.

Winter in Afghanistan

In the farthest corner of the long, high tent a paraffin lamp was burning on a bedside table where the veterans were playing cards. The lamp cast a purple shadow over the table on which the cards were dealt, over the faces of the players, over streams of cigarette smoke, and over the soldier who was standing motionless in the aisle between rows of bunk beds.

In the middle of the tent a round iron stove was roaring, and the few young soldiers sitting on stools next to it were waving around leggings that belonged to the old-timers. Toreadors on wooden horses – although it's hard to imagine a toreador willing to wash someone else's leggings . . .

Some of the men were dozing, half-on, half-off their beds, while others were talking idly among themselves; two soldiers had found a place near the card-players and were sewing little strips of white material into the collars of cotton field jackets. A pudgy soldier, his booted feet resting on his bed frame and his hands thrust under his head, was lying back, staring up at the netting of the bunk above him, singing. Everything he sang was to the same tune, and he sang every song in the same quiet, uninflected voice – he sang mechanically, thinking of other things.

The tent was hot and muggy and smelled of firelighters, tobacco, dirty clothes. The soldiers had eaten not long before and now, full and satisfied, were waiting for the nightly roll call.

The pudgy soldier was singing, 'No fence, no garden, no familiar face . . . There's no vodka, no women, won't ever be any . . .'

The toreadors were furiously fanning the stove with their rags, and to one side it was beginning to glow an angry red.

A couple of men were already snoring.

Cards flicked against the little table. The veterans were playing 'Joker', smoking, making jokes, not paying any attention at all to the soldier standing nearby.

'Looks as if I'll stick,' said a broad-shouldered young red-head in a tattered field jacket. He had a large, hairy chest, a small head, long arms. They called him 'Udmurt of Phnom-Penh'. He was a Russian from the Udmurt Republic whom the old-timers from the tour before his had nicknamed 'Udmurt', and for some reason 'from Phnom-Penh' too. Even now he was still called that behind his back.

'And this time I'll fold,' a small, swarthy, fine-featured soldier said angrily – Sanko, a Belorussian whose last name really was Sanko. He threw his last card, a ten of clubs, onto the table.

'Ah,' said Ostapenkov, 'I'll take that.'

'You'll take that,' muttered Udmurt from Phnom-Penh, 'and so these come out.' He quickly put two cards down on the table.

The lithe, skinny, big-eared Tatar Ivanov fixed his clear round eyes on the cards, bit his narrow lips between his sharp white teeth, and covered Udmurt's two cards with the six of clubs and the queen of hearts.

Udmurt glanced at the wide-eyed queen with flowing hair, and announced, 'She reminds me of someone.'

'Valechka,' said Ostapenkov.

'Valechka's hair is darker,' Sanko retorted.

'But she has the same eyes, like a lamb's,' Ostapenkov said.

Ivanov was left with the jokers. He picked up the deck of cards and began to shuffle them fluidly with his strong, dry, long fingers. Ostapenkov rooted through his pockets, found his cigarettes, lit one off the lamp, inhaled, and tried to blow a smoke ring. On the second attempt he succeeded.

'Charlie Chaplin,' he began, 'left a million to whoever could make twelve smoke rings, blow a stream of smoke through them, then make that stream turn into a smoke ring too. He was one hell of a smoker.'

'Crazy . . .' said Udmurt. 'Twelve.'

'Yes, but what if you practised?' Sanko picked up a cigarette, lit it, and started to blow out thick batches of smoke without managing to produce a single ring.

'You might be okay at it by the time you've spent the million on smokes,' said Ostapenkov, grinning.

'Still, a million . . .' Udmurt from Phnom-Penh said in a soft voice.

'One million,' Ostapenkov repeated. He paused, glanced quickly at the soldier in the aisle, and in a different voice demanded, 'You have something to tell us, Dulya?'

The soldier in the aisle – his last name, Stodolya, had been changed into Dulya – looked at the lamp and said nothing. He was a young man, docile, into whom a simple truth had been beaten, since his very first days of service with the company, the way it had been beaten into every other kid, with fists: if you spit at the group it will wipe itself clean, but if the group spits at you you'll drown.

The group was divided into three castes: the sparrows, the

spooners, and the old-timers. The first had six months under their belts, the second a year, the third a year and a half. Kids and demobs didn't belong to any caste: the first were beneath the group, under its heels, and the second were somewhere off to the side, on the periphery. By long-standing convention the demobs could order a filter-tip cigarette or a cup of water brought to their beds in the middle of the night, but they didn't abuse the custom; in general they acted with a certain degree of reserve, and more often than not they tried to keep their voices down – they were living out their last weeks in the barracks, whose masters, as everyone clearly knew, were the old-timers, who still had six more months to serve, who could suddenly turn angry, recall old grievances, and, rallying the whole group to their side, avenge themselves with their fists against the demobs. It had happened before in the camp.

The group lived by its own special rules, though no one knew when or by whom they had been thought up. At the root of the rules lay one dialectical formula: everything is in flux, everything changes, and even the newest nobody eventually became an old-timer – it was as inevitable as the collapse of imperialism. It was difficult to raise an argument against it and certainly nobody did. That wasn't allowed. Which was also one of the rules: Keep quiet unless someone asks you something. Asking questions was a right reserved to members of the higher castes. And if you were asked a question you had to answer. That was another rule, and it was now being broken by the big-nosed, big-eyed soldier nicknamed Dulya.

He was standing in the aisle, looking at the lamp, silent.

'You still have . . .' Ostapenkov glanced at his watch – forty minutes to go until lights out – '. . . half an hour.'

'We know, we know!' said Sanko. 'Another hand?'

Sanko put a card down on the table.

Ivanov covered it. 'I know . . .' He fell silent for a moment, casting a sidelong look a Dulya. 'I know certain facts. *Facts*,' he repeated.

'Really?' Ostapenkov asked.

'Yes.' Ivanov drummed his fingernails on the little table. 'But later, later.'

'Don't hold back, tell us,' Sanko said impatiently.

Ivanov shook his head.

'Let's hear the story he's got for us.' The pudgy soldier who sang to himself dropped his feet to the wood-planked floor with a crash, threw on his oilskin, and left the tent. After a few minutes he came back, his oilskin dripping with rain. He took it off in the doorway and shook it dry. He went over to his bunk, hung the oilskin on the bed frame, and resumed his former position, only this time with his wet, clay-crusted boots on the floor instead of up on the rail. He lay down, not saying anything, and then started another song: 'No more running, no more jumping, no more singing, no more loving; my drunken youth has swirled away into the mist . . .'

The soldier nicknamed Dulya stood in front of the card-players, his shoulders involuntarily slumped and his legs crossing now this way, now that. He was looking at the lamp, whose light seemed hot to him, and though his eyes were aching he would not take them off the flame behind its cloudy glass. It was easier to keep quiet when he stared at it. For some time he had felt that way, or at least it felt like some time.

'Water,' said Udmurt, his eyes on his cards.

Dulya gladly went off to get it – dinner had consisted of oversalted pearl barley and stringy, oversalted pork, and he was dying of thirst. The metal tank of drinking-water stood on a table near the tent's entrance. He turned the tap, got the water, gulped a cupful, and wanted to drink some more but Udmurt shouted out, 'What's keeping you over there, you giving birth?' Dulya poured out some more water, returned, and handed the cup to Udmurt, who swallowed it greedily.

Dulya went back to standing motionless in the aisle. Again the yellow light of the lamp began to stream into his eyes.

She's nothing anyway, he thought, and was suddenly struck with shame. He felt ashamed for thinking it, ashamed for imagining that she was here, in the long, shadowy tent, that she was standing somewhere nearby and, understanding nothing, staring at him . . .

'Twenty minutes to go,' Ostapenkov said.

Dulya fixed his eyes on him.

'What are you looking at?'

'Hit him in the head, he'll tell you,' said Udmurt.

'There's still time for that,' Ostapenkov answered. He wanted to add that things weren't so simple, but he didn't say anything; that would be too much of a compliment to the kid Dulya. He'd already been paid enough attention as it was. Since they'd read the letter no one had so much as lifted a finger against Dulya, even though he'd flagrantly violated one of the rules – he hadn't answered his elders' questions. If it hadn't been for Ostapenkov the others would of course have thrashed him long before. But Ostapenkov wouldn't let them. For the time being he had begun to take an interest in the matter – there was something significant, something terrifying behind all this. They always grilled the new men, punished them, bled them dry, so to speak, to find out everything: what their lives had been like back home, what their work had been, how many girls they'd had, the hair colour, the eye colour of their sisters, relatives, cousins, how many litres they'd drunk before they were inducted into the army. From the married men they would extract the secrets of their first married night. Could anything be more intimate, more terrifying than one's first night of marriage? But now Ostapenkov sensed that yes, there could be, and the thought astonished him.

'Hey, Dulya, just watch it,' Ostapenkov said, shuffling the cards. He'd lost this time.

'Should we let him sit down?' Ivanov asked. 'You're tired, aren't you? Want to sit down?'

Dulya nodded his head uncertainly.

Ivanov sighed. 'Well, keep standing then.'

When they heard the joke, Udmurt, Sanko, and the other soldiers burst out laughing. Ostapenkov didn't. The kid's stubbornness was beginning to annoy him.

The game continued.

The stove sang its endless hymns of fire. Rain was beating on the tent. Outside it was winter, snowless, muddy, wet, with cold fogs in the morning and icy midday winds.

It was quiet, the war in wintertime. The regiment rarely went out on operations. Tanks got bogged down on the steppes, let alone wheeled vehicles. Even the rebels preferred to rest – the paths and passes through the high mountains were choked with snow.

Winter was almost peaceful, although sometimes some dead-keen officer or other would throw his detachment out on road patrol somewhere in the green zone, whose vast stretches of vineyards were white and impassable for the whole season. Or a mine would explode under some wheeled vehicle bringing flour or canned food to the regiment from Kabul. Which didn't compare at all to the war during the summer, when the regiment conducted one operation after another. In the summer, over every sort of terrain, in ravines, on heights that stretched into the clouds, in the desert sands, in ancient green earthen towns, in secluded *kishlak*s – everywhere there was gunfire, everywhere explosions of mines and grenades, glittering bursts of tracer at night, columns raising billows of dust, houses collapsing, fields of grain being trampled to the ground. The summer was hot, and reeked of absinthe, and on the sides of the road lay black hulks of recently destroyed vehicles and fly-matted, swollen, foul-smelling camels with whitened eyes. The summer was hot.

But for now it was winter and the soldiers busied themselves with peaceful chores, grew fatter, ruddier, paler.

Ten minutes remained until lights out. Dulya had to say 'yes' or 'no', but he remained silent. He was afraid to confess – he knew that until his very last day they would not let him have a moment's peace. He was well aware of what happens when the attention of the whole group falls on one man alone. There were a few 'perpetual' kids in the regiment: one had tried to shoot himself, another had drunk the urine of a yellow-fever victim in order to get himself a few months in the hospital, a third had broken down, sobbing, on his first operation. They were laughing-stocks, and not only in their own group either: the entirety of the group had noticed them, knew who they were. Any fledgling sparrow could accost a 'perpetual' kid, call him names, tweak his ears, kick him, or force him to sweep the barracks or clean out the latrines. 'Perpetual' kids were always caked with mud and riddled with lice, yet they got used to their particular position, even came to see it as natural – probably had to, if they were to keep on living.

But his tongue couldn't even manage to form itself around the word 'no'. And if I don't say anything it will mean 'yes', he thought, horrified.

And then that letter. He hadn't managed to destroy it in time and Ivanov had taken it from him. She had had a bad dream and then written him that letter, which was like a prayer, with the word 'God' in every sentence. The old-timers had fallen on Dulya with questions but he remained silent.

Sometimes a comforting thought came to him: I didn't write that letter – *she* did.

The longer he kept quiet the harder it would be to remain so, and the more horrifying it would be to say anything. It would be best not to think of anything or anyone, to remember nothing. But . . .

In the heavy sunlit air flecks of down were soaring over passers-by, newspaper stands, cars; the down flew obliquely between houses, its fluffy cheeks brushing their hot and rough stone walls, snagging on the jagged edges of windowsills, floating effortlessly inside through every open pane. He wanted to close the window but she said no, leave it, and the window stayed open, and the down flew through it into the house.

While she was making coffee in the kitchen he wandered along the bookshelves that took up two whole walls in the room; it was the library of her father, who worked as a baker at a breadmaking plant. The numerous books were all old, dog-eared, heavy, sober-looking. His eyes were caught by one with a black rose on its spine, and when he opened it he discovered that it was a collection of Chinese poetry from the T'ang dynasty. He found the titles of the poems funny: 'I Picture what I see from my Grass-roofed Hut'; 'I Will Arise Early'; 'A Poem in Five Hundred Words about what was in My Soul as I Travelled from the Capital to Fin-sian'; 'On a Spring Night I Rejoice for the Rain.' They were like the poplar-seed flecks that clung trustingly to the grey walls of the houses, like a little girl running off from her mother to greet strangers passing by, like a man walking down a crowded street who thinks of something funny, cannot control his lips, his eyes, his cheeks, and breaks into a smile. The poets had names that rustled, rang, and whispered: Yan Tsun, Wan Wei, Liu Yan-tsin. One was like a gentle wind or the breathing of someone who's asleep: Du Fu.

They read them aloud. At first they took turns, but when he said it the results were poor.

> With the wine of Szechuan
> I would dispel my sad thoughts –
> Only I don't have a farthing
> And no one will lend me one.

He read that, but it came out as flat and banal as a teenager complaining to a friend about his parents refusing to buy him a pair of jeans or a cassette player. He felt the truth of the image and refused to read any more. Then she read, and the poems became exactly what they were meant to be: sighs, tears, spring rain, lamentations, grass, birds, mountains, towers, trees, water-falls, snowflakes the size of mats. She began to read a poem by Du Fu, 'The New Bride's Farewell':

> In spring the morning glory's shoots
> Are utterly fragile.
> And so it is with me:
> When a soldier is married in the village
> It's too soon to rejoice . . .

She suddenly fell silent, hung her head, and closed the book, which started to shake in her hands. He kissed her pale fingers, which were clutching the book's cover, and she burst into tears.

It was only July then, he still had two and a half months ahead of him, he was planning on enrolling in the institute, he wasn't really thinking about the army at all, much less the war, but she was crying and going on about how it was all so terrible, terrible. But why, why, he asked, and she answered: I don't know, stop pestering me, go away, you're keeping me from studying.

It was only July, the beginning of July; he was spending his days with his textbooks, getting ready for the entrance exams, and he saw the future clearly: they would spend five years in the auditoriums and libraries of the institute, then they'd go off to some faraway village, amidst pine needles and blue-grey hills. They would have their house and garden, the garden blossoming white in the spring, and on autumn mornings they would stop to gather apples in a basket: that was it. It was true that she didn't want to live in the countryside, but he was determined on it. While only in his second year of high school he had read *The Life of the Archpriest Arrakum*, and from then on he had been consumed by a desire to dedicate his life to something. Exactly how to go about doing that he wasn't sure, and he was tormented by the thought that he would never find it, that his life would be tedious and wasted. But in his heart smouldered the sermons of that indomitable man:

'In my sadness I pondered what to do – preach the word of God or run away somewhere? Because my wife and children had bound me.

'And seeing my grief, my wife approached me cautiously and asked me, My Lord, what is making you grieve?

'I told her: Wife, what should I do? There is a winter of heresy abroad – should I speak or remain silent? You have bound me!

'And she said: Lord have mercy! What are you saying, Petrovich? I myself have heard you read the Apostle's words: Art thou bound unto a wife? Seek not to be loosed.

Art thou loosed from a wife? Seek not a wife. The children and
I give you our blessing: dare . . .'

And only towards the end of his schooldays, when he read
about the Populists who had gone off to teach in the countryside,
did he find that something.

They were still preparing for their entrance exams but they
discussed the future as if they were getting their degrees the next
day or the day after. She proposed a compromise: they would
work for only three years in the countryside, the minimum time
the regulations demanded, and then come back. But the
inflexible Petrovich was whispering something else in his ear,
arguing that he would have to go for ever, until the grave, and
live in the sticks to educate the benighted people – electrification
plus television notwithstanding. It was for that very reason, when
he thought about his future life in the country, that he fell in love
with the white garden and the wooden house with its wide
windows and its big stove solid as a medieval keystone.

The white specks of fluff were sailing through the windows,
tumbling over one another, and ahead of him were five years of
study at the institute, then a long life in the house surrounded by
its white garden – but she had shut the book and was crying.

He wasn't accepted into the institute.

He flinched when he heard the sharp sound of Ostapenkov
dropping his cards onto the little table.

'Well then, have you swallowed your tongue?' Ostapenkov
asked him through clenched teeth.

'Christ, even a goat would understand,' said Sanko. 'Why
won't he talk? And his old lady's letter with god for every other
word, Christ. We should tell the Zampolit and the captain.'

Ostapenkov cut him off. 'No, we can sort this out ourselves.

He won't keep silent. We'll loosen his tongue somehow or other
– damned if we don't.'

'But even a goat would understand,' Sanko repeated.

'We're not goats,' answered Ostapenkov, tightening his
muscles.

'Well then, that's it,' the Tatar Ivanov pronounced softly and
resolutely. He raised his bright round eyes and fixed them on
Dulya. 'We had a Baptist on our logging team once,' he added
unhurriedly. 'Or maybe he was a Seventh-Day Adventist.'

Udmurt started to laugh.

'Anyway, a true believer,' Ivanov continued. 'I know the kind,
I've studied them. For example, you're drunk and you say to him
the first thing that pops into your head, and, like a virgin before
her first abortion, he – '

'Then she isn't a virgin,' noted Udmurt.

' – before her first abortion, he goes pale and starts to tremble.
He answers: Why did you say that, what makes you behave this
way?'

'And then you nail him,' Udmurt said.

Ivanov shrugged his shoulders in disgust. 'Bah, just get your
hands dirty.'

'You said facts,' Ostapenkov said impatiently. 'What facts?'

'Facts you shall have. Alyokha!' Ivanov shouted. 'Get over
here!'

One of the toreadors broke away from his little table, a round,
swarthy runt of a boy. He came up, stopped, sniffed through his
snub nose, looked around with moist eyes at the old-timers, and
loudly said, 'Here!'

'Look at them,' Ivanov prompted.

Everyone took a look at the two kids.

'So, Alyokha, how's things? How's life treating you?'

Alyokha glanced at him inquiringly and, having read something or another in his eyes, answered in an almost offhand voice, 'They fuck us, but we're becoming men!'

Everyone burst out laughing.

'All right, Alyokha, you can go,' Ivanov said with a good-natured smile. 'You see?' he asked his comrades.

'Course we saw, but so what?' Sanko said.

Ivanov looked at him with a fatherly reproach.

'Long ago I noticed – I noticed from the very first – that this Dulya, this Dulyette, wasn't like the others. All the kids are like kids, but . . . Well, here's your first fact,' he said ominously. 'Who has heard Dulya swear? Who' – he raised his voice – 'who remembers Dulya cursing at anyone?'

Everyone in the tent fell silent; the inquisitive were all straining towards the site of the trial. The old-timers were walking right up and settling themselves, grinning, on beds and tables; even the spooners were moving in closer. The kids and sparrows were listening from a little way off, craning their necks and timidly catching one another's eyes.

'There,' said Ivanov. 'That was the first fact. The second. Whenever someone is hit, taught to have some brains, Dulya's eyes are like a virgin's before her first abortion – '

The door to the tent opened slightly and the orderly's head appeared. 'Duty officer!' the wide-eyed head shouted hoarsely before disappearing again.

The toreadors picked themselves up from the tables and started rushing around the tent, using leggings to disperse the tobacco smoke. The spooners and old-timers – who by the rules could sit or lie down on their bunks fully dressed – stood up, straightened their beds, and sidled off into the corners.

'Hand those back!' shouted Udmurt in a desperate whisper, and the kids raced to return the leggings, which were warm and almost dry.

The door opened and, stooping over to avoid hitting his head on the lintel, into the tent stepped a lieutenant.

'Compan-ee!' the duty sergeant shouted wildly. 'Attenn – '

'Stand at ease,' the lieutenant said, straightening up and walking into the middle of the tent. He was tall, well-built, and narrow-shouldered, with dark sardonic eyes, hard thin lips, a cleft chin, a small but full moustache, and a scar running from his left ear to his Adam's apple.

He looked around, turned to the roaring stove and shook his head.

'Damp it down,' he said casually. A spooner twisted the valve to the fuel tank shut.

'You've been warned already,' said the lieutenant.

A week before, the regiment had been informed that a platoon from a unit stationed near Kandahar had been burned to a crisp in its tent: the orderlies and guards had fallen asleep and burning fuel had leaked out of the stove and spread across the wood-planked floor of the tent.

His eyes still on the scarlet side of the stove, the lieutenant asked the soldier standing behind him, 'Vorontsov, what's that in your hand?'

'Nothing, comrade lieutenant,' the soldier answered innocently. Vorontsov was Alyokha's last name.

The lieutenant sighed. 'Nothing now – but what was it before?'

'Nothing.'

'Ostapenkov, come over here,' the lieutenant said in a dull voice.

Ostapenkov walked to the middle of the tent and the lieutenant turned to face him.

'Come on, say it: "Comrade lieutenant, private first class

Osta-a-penkov at your orders." We're not on the kolkhoz anymore, are we?'

'Comrade lieutenant . . .' Ostapenkov started to say with an embarrassed smile.

The lieutenant interrupted him. 'What did Vorontsov hand over to you?'

'Nothing. To me, nothing.'

'To whom, then? You, Udmurt?'

'Absolutely not, sir!' Udmurt bellowed.

'Vorontsov,' said the lieutenant. 'There I am, let's just suppose, walking down the street in your village. Let's say I run into you, Vorontsov. You're with a girl, you're wearing a tie – '

Vorontsov grimaced. 'I don't wear ties, Christ.'

'Don't spout off unless you're asked something,' Ivanov whispered loudly.

'So let's suppose I run into you. With a girl. No tie – you're in a denim suit. Have you saved up enough coupons to get a denim suit yet?'

'No.'

'How come? Everyone else has. What have you done with it all? They took it off you, eh?'

'No, I spent it on shit,' Vorontsov muttered quickly.

'Christ, on shit,' repeated the lieutenant, frowning.

'Baa, at the bakery, on jam, on, er . . .'

'Stop bleating, you're not in a stable,' Ivanov said in another loud whisper.

'Fine. So I run into you, take off my shoes, peel off my tattered socks that haven't been washed in a year, hand them to you, and say, Quick, wash these and wring them dry or I'll piss on you and wring *you* dry.'

Everyone burst into laughter.

'How would you answer me then? You'd belt me between the eyes and that would be that. Right?'

'Him against you, no chance,' said one of the old-timers.

'So he might whistle to his little friends or pick up a sledgehammer. Right?'

His eyes filled with devotion, Vorontsov looked at the lieutenant and answered, 'No.'

The lieutenant smiled. 'Well, maybe not me – someone else. What's the difference. Maybe Stodolya, for instance. How would you have answered him?'

Vorontsov glanced at Stodolya. 'Him? He-he-he.'

'Exactly. The same with all these other shits – why don't you tell them all to go to hell? Whose leggings were you washing?' the lieutenant said severely. 'Tell me or you're off to the cooler.'

'What for?' Vorontsov cried desperately.

'For your own good. And why does it reek of smoke in here? You, Stodolya, were you smoking?'

Everyone burst into laughter again: Stodolya was the one non-smoker in the company.

'Were you?'

Stodolya shook his head.

'Not you, then who? Come on, answer me!'

Stodolya looked at him without saying anything.

'Why won't you speak?'

Everything became deathly quiet.

'I don't know. I didn't see,' Stodolya answered at last in a metallic voice.

'Of course. How would you know? Your head is filled with any old nonsense, anything but duty, you don't take any notice at all of reality, so to speak. You're asleep on your feet. What do I have to do, talk to each one of you in the corner? So that no one else sees, no one else hears? Is that it? Or are you going to start sending me anonymous notes? Is that the new routine? No one knows anything, no one hears anything, people are set up, no one says anything, their noses are broken, they're given black eyes, and they say: I fell, I was walking along, I slipped, and when I woke up – a black eye! Well one day I'll put the lot of you on a charge! Don't smirk, Ostapenkov, you're the first one into the disciplinary battalion!' The lieutenant fell silent and glanced at his watch. 'Regimental roll call is cancelled,' he said.

The soldiers broke into a joyous buzz.

'The rain. And New Year's coming up. So . . . Well, is everyone more or less here? Who's on duty tonight? Topady – Topady, who will be your sentries?'

Sergeant Topady called out three names.

'All of them new kids again. It won't do. Let's try it once more – Udmurt will go on duty, and Ivanov and Zharov. Any questions?' The lieutenant looked at his watch once more and headed towards the exit. 'Lights out in half an hour. I'll come back to check, and if I find any one of you in a vertical position I'll whip him – you'll only have yourself to blame. To work, sentries, and no more nonsense. That'll be all.'

'I'm not going on guard duty,' said Zharov, the pudgy soldier who sang to himself all night. He was a demob, the last of the Mohicans: all of his friends had gone back to Russia a month earlier, but he had been forced to stay behind after a fight with a staff officer.

The staff officer had taken to sitting in the officers' latrine at night in order to catch, through a crack in the door, glimpses of a curly-haired head that appeared fleetingly over the top of gossamer curtains in a lighted window opposite the latrine. Valya, a typist in the headquarters pool, had a rich assortment of prospects in the regiment, and the staff officer – not handsome, undersized, rather the worse for wear – didn't exactly shine among them. So at night he would sit in the latrine across from her window. One fateful evening the staff officer fell into a state of great excitement after he caught sight, through the gossamer curtains, of her white breasts and a bit of her stomach. He woke up in the middle of the night, tossing and turning, and couldn't manage to get back to sleep. He was tormented by those breasts with their dark nipples, by that bit of white stomach. The staff officer got up, dressed, and, not knowing exactly why, went out to stand underneath Valechka's window, which as it turned out was slightly ajar. He opened the shutters, climbed halfway into the room, and the first thing he saw, glowing white in the darkness, was a pair of panting bodies. One of the bodies leaped up, and the staff officer fell down from the windowsill, blood pouring from his nose onto his uniform. Without a word, he got up, again climbed halfway into the window, then tumbled back out along with the half-dressed soldier. They rolled around on the ground, wheezing and throwing punches. Valechka closed her window and watched them, biting her lips, and groaned in exasperation. While out to answer a call of nature, a tank commander spotted them and, thinking that the enemy had infiltrated the camp, raced off to the officers' quarters to sound the alarm. During the investigation, which was conducted by the chief of staff himself, the staff officer lied: He had seen someone trying to open the window, he caught the burglar, and so the fight broke out. Valechka repeated over and over that she didn't know anything, that this was the first time she had laid eyes on either the soldier or the staff officer – she had been asleep, she had heard noises, shouts, gunshots. Zharov talked all manner of nonsense to save Valechka's reputation, which had been irretrievably sunk long ago. In the end the chief of staff put an end to the matter, brought the inquest to a close, and severely reprimanded Valechka and the staff officer. But he demoted

Sergeant Zharov, threw him in the cooler for ten days, and promised him that he'd be seeing the New Year in with the regiment and not back home.

'Don't be a goat, Zharov,' the lieutenant said softly. 'You know I would have let you go a long time ago, but . . . If it was up to me you could loaf around for days on end. But command is interested to know if you're pulling your weight or just kicking pears off a tree. Judge for yourself – I can't very well lie.'

'I'm not going on guard duty,' the ex-sergeant repeated in an indifferent voice. He took off his belt. 'Write a memo to the head of the disciplinary tribunal.'

'It's not too warm in the cooler this time of year.'

'Write it,' Zharov said sullenly.

'You're beginning to annoy me.'

'Write it.'

'You think I won't?'

'Write it.'

'Fine, you still have plenty of time left to rot in the cooler.' The lieutenant gave in. 'It'll weigh on my conscience,' he sighed, then said, 'Aminzhonov, you'll be the third. And no fooling around!' he said loudly to everyone else.

The soldiers answered him with a delighed roar, and the lieutenant went back out into the rain knowing that the men loved him more than ever.

The card-players returned to their places, struck matches, and started to smoke. Zharov undressed, lay down, and covered himself with his flannel blanket even though Lights Out wasn't for another half an hour. Alyokha Vorontsov filled three battered green pots with water and placed them on the stove, which had fallen silent but was now starting to clatter again – the valve had been given a spirited twist counterclockwise.

Ivanov and Udmurt were furious; they weren't at all pleased about being assigned sentry duty. Ostapenkov walked over to Alyokha Vorontsov, who was sitting next to the stove with a cellophane packet of captured tea. Sensing the worst, Alyokha stood up, a sorry grimace on his face. He prepared himself to carry out the order, 'Heart to arms!' This strange command never sounded strange to anyone who received it: to obey it all one had to do was stick out one's chest and take a punch on the second button down from the top of one's shirt. In the baths it was immediately obvious which kids and sparrows were the stupidest and slowest: in the middle of their chests, all blue and black, were 'Orders of Fools' – bruises. Vorontsov readied himself for a blow to the heart, since after all he had blundered three times: he hadn't managed to give back the old-timers' leggings in time, he had spouted nonsense without being asked, and he had said 'baa' as though he was in a stable.

But Ostapenkov put his hand on Vorontsov's shoulder and said, 'Sit down, brew us some strong tea.'

'Yes, sir!'

Ostapenkov fell silent, then suddenly asked him, 'Listen, would you give Dulya a couple of punches?'

'Dulya?'

'Yes.'

'Why?'

'Because. If we really, really asked you to. As an experiment.'

Vorontsov blinked in confusion and muttered, 'But why? There has to be a reason . . .'

'We'll find one.'

'Really? I don't know . . . If it's absolutely necessary . . .'

'It is. We'll come for you later, then,' said Ostapenkov. 'Make the tea and then get into bed. We'll wake you when it's time.'

Ostapenkov walked back to his spot, where Ivanov, Udmurt, Sanko, a few other old-timers, and two spooners, both friends with the old-timers, were waiting.

'So where is that clown?' Ostapenkov asked.

'Not here. Probably went to the bog,' said one of the spooners.

'And who authorized him?' Ostapenkov asked. He called to the duty sergeant, who said that Boiko and Sarakyesyan had asked permission to go, but not Dulya. Ostapenkov's face contorted: what Dulya had done was in itself already unheard of, since every kid and sparrow was required to say where and for how long he was going to be away on personal errands, which as a rule meant a trip to the latrines and nothing else. True, sparrows were allowed to visit friends from home in other units or to go to the library, but kids were free to do neither. Although a trip to the library was permitted under one condition – that the kid could recite the guard regulations by heart. It goes without saying that no one passed the test.

'Come on, drop it,' Ivanov said. 'He's no grass. I've studied his sort and that much is obvious.'

'So he'll just walk back in and not mention it,' Sanko said quietly, trying to recall if he'd ever hit Dulya or merely sworn at him.

'Let him try,' Udmurt said, scratching his hairy chest.

'He just forgets that he's only a kid,' Ivanov said.

Ostapenkov lit a cigarette, inhaled the smoke, and pensively twisted the spent match in his fingers.

'And if he doesn't mention it, then what?' Sanko asked.

'Drop it, you lot,' said the second spooner.

'He's sitting in the shithouse,' and old-timer suggested.

They fell silent.

'How long until Lights Out?' asked Sanko.

Ostapenkov looked at him sullenly. 'We'll tear him apart first.'

Ten minutes passed, twenty, and Boiko and Sarakyesyan returned from the latrines. They hadn't seen Dulya.

'Get the kids and sparrows into bed,' Ostapenkov said. 'We'll see this thing through. Call the Lights Out, Topady.'

The Moldavian duty sergeant looked at his watch and barked, 'Lights Out!'

The company began to get ready for bed: the sparrows hastily, the spooners leisurely, the kids lightning-fast – a thunder of boots, clanking belt buckles, and creaking mattress-springs.

The old-timers and the two spooners drank their black tea, sweating and breathing noisily. With the tea they had biscuits and sugar. The biscuits smelled like mould, as did everything else in winter: tea, dried noodles, soup, powdered potatoes, bread. If you had a connection in the canteen you didn't eat bread but brought biscuits back to your mess. The bread was baked in the camp, and the loaves were dense, flat, coarse, coffee-coloured, reeking of bleach, and very sour: they left everyone in an agony of heartburn that sometimes led to vomiting. The officers ate another kind of bread – wheat bread, fully risen, soft, light-coloured: officers' bread. Decent flour and strong yeast rarely made it to the camp. War is war.

'No. It wouldn't do him any good,' Ivanov said. 'The brass wouldn't look at him twice – a grass and a believer at that.'

'My brother was telling me,' the first spooner recalled, 'that someone like that turned up on his ship – my brother was in the navy – and they got him transferred to shore duty.'

'That's it?'

'That's it. Believers join up – it's usually the Baptists who refuse. Easier to go to prison than carry a gun . . . the goats. Just means this bloke isn't a Baptist, that's all.'

'But what did we ever do to him that was so bad?' asked Sanko. 'Christ, I never even touched him. Yelled at him a bit, like

at the others, but what the hell, are we supposed to treat him like
a lord? Everyone has to go through the same thing. They're lucky
they never ran across Khan. Did we ever crush cigarette butts
out on his heels or smash his teeth in? Do you remember when
Khan tied up that gypsy and made everyone spit in his face?'

'Nearly drowned him. That gypsy's probably hitting our
columns now, the bastard. We've got to get him,' said one of the
old-timers.

'Khan's hitting something now too – hitting a piss-pot
somewhere around Vorkuta.'

'We should catch that damn gypsy.'

'Most likely he's swilling whisky in Chicago.'

Sanko stood up, yawned loudly, and said, 'Well then.'

Ostapenkov cut him short. 'Where you off to?'

'Bed. I haven't been sleeping too well,' Sanko answered, sitting
down on his bunk.

'You can catch up in the train on the way to see Khan in
Vorkuta. You'll sleep soundly enough,' Udmurt laughed.

'Let's go and find him,' said Ostapenkov.

'This rain,' the second spooner muttered dejectedly.

Ostapenkov turned to face him. 'I didn't quite catch what
business you had here.'

'We're, uh . . .' The spooner smiled weakly.

'Let's get to bed, Seryoga,' the first spooner said to him. Both
of them moved off, smiling wanly.

'I don't think he ran off specifically to spill the beans, either,'
said Ostapenkov.

'Which means . . .'

'One of two things: he's with some friend from home – or he's
skulking around the regimental CP.'

'I'm going to tear that sneak in half, I'm – ' Udmurt stopped
cold. 'Did you hear that?'

There was the sound of another explosion, followed moments later by yet another. The soldiers went out into the roadway, into the rain and darkness.

'Mortars,' a guard said. 'They're hitting the first battery.'

At the edge of the camp flames were blazing in the pitch dark and dull thumps were reverberating – the battery responding with howitzers.

'Let's just hope there's no alert,' said Sanko.

More shells burst and a chorus of howitzers answered them: Boom! Boom! B-B-Boom! Strings of tracer rose red at the edge of the camp, intersecting each other before fading away into the darkness. The rattle of automatic rifles could barely be distinguished from the incessant spatter of rain on the roof of the mushroom tent. Shells started bursting more rapidly, and then the heavy machine-guns and rapid-firing grenade-launchers opened up. The rain was pounding, the howitzers hammering 'Boom! Boom!' and the night exploded with a meaty crackle, scattering flames in every direction.

The old-timers went back into the tent and stood around the stove, smoking, silent. The probability of an alert weighed on them. They didn't want to fight in a winter rain at night, they just wanted to lie down under their blankets, to hell with everything, and plunge themselves into dreams of home.

'Shit,' Sanko said in a strange thin voice.

'What?' Ostapenkov asked him sharply.

'What! Fuck him, let him cart an icon around on his shirt if he wants to!'

'Yes?' Ostapenkov's eyes narrowed. 'And what if we have to fight with him tomorrow? And attack? Eh?'

'That's right,' agreed Ivanov.

'He'll run away for sure,' Ostapenkov continued. 'He'll throw down his gun, turn tail, and they'll jam a barrel rod through your eye while he snivels and saves his own skin. These Baptists and Adventists . . . they should all be sent to the North Pole so we don't have to breathe their stinking incense. Motherfuckers! Motherfuckers!'

'I know his kind. And I've been keeping my eye on that streak of piss for a long time,' said Ivanov. 'The way he looked at that prisoner . . .'

'He wants to keep his hands clean! But no way!' Ostapenkov clenched his fist. 'No way – better to hang himself right now. Either he's a hundred percent recce or he gets the hell out. In a recce company there's no place for angels.'

'Ostap.' All of a sudden a sarcastic voice was heard off to one side. 'Hey, Ostap.'

Ostapenkov whirled around, startled. The ex-sergeant, Zharov, was looking at him from between the bars of his bunk bed. He was lying under the covers, his hands clasped behind his head.

'Don't be scared, it's only me.'

'Me, scared? What, of you?' With an effort of will Ostapenkov tried to relax the muscles in his face, but the smile came out strained – cheeks twitching, lips quivering, eyebrows in motion – and his face hardened again almost instantly.

'Maybe right now you're not scared of me,' Zharov said in a conciliatory voice.

'I've never been afraid of you.'

'That's how it seems to you now. You're kidding yourself. From time to time I used to fool myself that I wasn't afraid of Khan. But I was scared of him, even though we were called up at the same time.' Zharov picked up a pack of cigarettes from the little table, took one out, lit it. 'I watched you there, taking that kid apart, and . . . Ostap, mind if I tell you something?'

'No.'

'You'll be sorry. Later.'

'Me?' Ostapenkov laughed.

The door creaked. Everyone turned to look and saw, in the entrance, a man with a darkened face. He stood in the doorway, dripping water, and behind him was the rustling, pounding, churning night. The guard shoved him in the back and closed the door from the outside. Stodolya said nothing. Everyone was looking at him, at his soaked and drooping trenchcoat, at his old, long since worn-out cap with its scorched earflaps, at his huge, tattered, mudstained leather boots, at his dark blue lips, his sharp wet nose, his sunken eyes.

'Get over there by the stove,' said Udmurt.

Ostapenkov glanced at Udmurt then again fixed his eyes on Stodolya. 'Ah,' he said in a hoarse voice, 'an apparition . . .'

Stodolya remained silent.

'Where have you been?' Ostapenkov asked him.

Stodolya raised his eyes, moved his lips.

'What? I can't hear you!'

'I believe in God,' Stodolya repeated.

The Belles

They brought us to the steppes; we saw tents, grey expanses, mountains on the horizon, and we came to live here: eating, sleeping, marching, falling ill with hepatitis and typhus, cleaning gun barrels, obeying officers, feeding fleas. We became sunburned, thin, we made friends, we stopped waking up at night when the forward posts opened fire on positions. We learned to smoke hash, to look doomed prisoners calmly in the eye, to not think of the future, to write dispassionate letters home.

There was a first day and a second, a twentieth, a sixtieth. The sun would float in the sky, the sky bright, the sun burning hot. We hated the sun: on operations, when the battery stayed out among the red sand dunes for days on end, the men from Vologda and Archangel got bloody noses.

It seemed that there was no time, only eternity. But when someone was carried to a helicopter under a sheet we would convince ourselves that time still existed for us, that eternity was that stretcher sailing off for ever. And we would think: Allow us to return for one moment to our villages and cities, and then let it happen – let them send us to eternity then, if it's so necessary. But most would leave straight from here, from these steppes, mountains, and deserts, and they would leave blackened, their shirts in tatters, barefoot.

Time passed, but slowly.

It was the hundredth day. In the sky steel lizards were flying around with metallic fruit in their claws. The sun was sucking the last drop of sweat from every pore, there was no water in the canteens, the water truck had slid into a ravine, dust lay in the riverbeds. A parched, parched land . . . Then the dappled lizards would appear, the ripe fruit would start to burst and slice to pieces the hides of pack camels, donkeys, and men: donkeys, men, and pack camels would bellow and the parched land would be irrigated, flooded. But the sun drank it all up immediately, and only rusted husks remained.

This is why, towards evening, that great yellow star grew heavy, sticky, troubled, and brown.

Time passed. It was the three-hundredth day; there still remained days and days, nights and nights, and sometimes I could see a little hill with a row of spruce trees, a church, gardens, peasant huts – I could see The Belles.

The Belles, not The Bells. On the steppes I savoured the melodiousness of this mistake, which is precisely what the peasants called and still call the village.

In The Belles there is a church with a tall steeple; there are neither icons nor windows in the church, birches and maples grow in the cupola, and the bell tower has no bell.

Up in the loft, poring over my books, I could look out of the dormer window and see the church, missing its cross but with its thin small spruces and its maple tree. People had knocked down the crosses, smashed every piece of glass, torn out its window-frames and doors, and would have taken the bricks too, had even chiselled away at its walls, but they had given up – Church masonry is solid. But trees don't give up, weeds and trees do their work, they scratch away at the cupola and the walls, day and night they grow and, working their fingers, make the cracks and chinks larger, and in winter every fissure and wrinkle is filled with ice and covered with snow: spring comes, and during the day the ice melts but at night it freezes – nature labours away tirelessly, building itself and beginning to destroy every work of human hands as soon as men lower their guard.

In autumn the little trees by the church were yellow, the maple crimson. From the loft window, before which stood a table with books, ashtrays, and a jar of kvass, I watched the church being devoured by nature, and it was easy for me to imagine it as a sort of Angkor Wat abandoned by the people because a flood had turned all the surrounding fields into a swamp and famine had broken out – like that royal city of the medieval Cambodian empire with its squares, temples, market-places, palaces, and colonnades punished by nature's right hand. Into the city stole the first wild shoots, loosening, gnawing at everything, and then the jungles rushed in, rushed in and engulfed Angkor Wat, the glory of Indochina.

I come to the little hill with its spruces and gardens and I drink water from the well, and no one sees me because everyone thinks I'm in the East, and they write letters to me there.

I meet the old man on the little hill and say: I'm back now, let's go home and have some tea. But he doesn't hear me.

The old man is a great lover of tea; he had developed a taste for it at the front, although people in Russian villages don't usually think much of the drink and make do with milk and kissel instead, which is more nourishing, more filling.

He made the tea expertly, and we sat over it for a long time, and I helped steer him towards his favourite theme, and he told me the usual mystic, eerie tale. How he went into the yard to do his business at the most dangerous and unpleasant hour, at midnight, how he went out and saw: the straw roof of the cowshed moving, splitting open, and a pair of legs appearing . . .

I tell him: grandfather, it's me, I've come back, let's go into the house, you'll play and sing. He doesn't hear; he's looking elsewhere.

It's true that the old man doesn't really know how to play, but there's an accordion in the house and, spurred on by the wine, he picks it up, draws strange melodies from it, and sings old convict songs: 'And across the mute mysterious taiga, the far Siberian lands, the tramp escaped from Sakhalin, along a narrow animal path . . .'

And then I slowly soar into the house, alone, and for fear of seeing them all together at once I climb up to the loft, where there is a chest, old-fashioned, strapped in iron around its corners. In the chest are all sorts of things: old, empty purses, glass beads, crumbling magazines about beekeeping, some handkerchiefs and rags, a few heavy church books. Before the war these books hadn't interested me much, for some reason . . .

The loft was my office, where I could read in peace or write long letters to friends, or to a hermit philosopher in the Baikal. The old man had written to me in the army to say that he had built me a studio out of logs near the bathhouse, and it made me sad to think that I wouldn't have to climb up to the loft for solitude any more, although it was only possible to sit there in the autumn or on rainy summer days – if the summer was hot the loft turned into an oven, a desert, like the copper bull where, in olden days, according to Gogol, the Poles used to put refractory Cossacks.

I could see a lot from the loft: churches, the street. Long ago it was the same Old Smolensk Road that the French had followed, pillaging villages on the way to Moscow, with bands coming out of the forests to spear them with pitchforks and hack at them with axes. I could also see the stand of spruce near the school – seven or eight spruce, tall and dark, over which the autumn sky was often incredibly brilliant, and looking at their tops against the brilliant sky I would vividly recall the Baikal, where I had met a woman from The Belles. I had managed to see a few things before the war, and it was easier for me than for those who hadn't.

I could see all that and the birch forest too. The view from the window was limited and blocked by bushes. But from the studio next to the bathhouse I could barely see any of it. Just the garden.

But that was beautiful too.

I remember the garden glowing under the autumn moon.

All day long under the yellow lime trees – and above them, in the bluest of skies, the falling sun was burning and blazing – the old man and I had been splitting birch wood. There were also pieces of aspen branches that the old man was cracking with a sharp hatchet while I shattered birch logs with a heavy maul – the birch was dense and knotted. We finished towards evening and went into the house, where our labours were rewarded with drink. And the old man picked up his accordion to sing: 'And across the mute mysterious taiga . . .' But I went outside to smoke, in the garden.

I walked by the still-flowering cosmos and phloxes; from the autumn flowers there wafted a faint draught, a thin, barely perceptible aroma. I circled around the house and saw the whole garden under the moonlight. I saw the asparagus bush speckled with the quicksilver of roses; I saw innumerable dully glowing apples throwing off a greenish light in the dark foliage.

I cast a glance at the lime trees beyond the fence, where a little pile of birch offcuts was burning silently and feebly. And over the bathhouse roof, with its severe black chimney, hung the Big Dipper.

I remember the garden in spring. I got up before dawn; brewing tea I rattled a spoon, dropped a saucer, and woke up the woman, who came out of our room, frowning angrily, and said that I was going to rouse the whole house because of my idiotic fishing; I offered her tea but she refused and, yawning, she left. I drank the tea, grabbed my cigarettes and a piece of bread, slipped out into the hallway, found a fishing pole and a jar of worms, quietly opened the door, and carefully descended the front steps, which didn't creak at all. In the garden I saw the mist, and in the mist apple and cherry trees in bloom. The branches and tree trunks were dark, the mist grey, the flowers white. The soft, turned earth in the vegetable garden was black; the seeds had already taken and little green shoots were coming up here and there.

I stood in the middle of the hazy, early-morning garden with my fishing pole, and all of a sudden it struck me as, yes, idiotic . . . I put the pole down on the grass, went up to the window behind which the woman was sleeping on a couch, and drummed my fingers on the windowpane. The house was divided into three rooms by thin plywood partitions, and I was afraid that everyone would hear me and, deciding that some pilgrim had appeared – there are still pilgrims wandering around Old Russia, and more than one tattered old man or wrinkled old woman had called at the house at The Belles before, with no family, no roots, no identity card, to spend the night and in the morning get some bread and treacle for the road – they would think that one of these visitors had knocked, and they would all come out to greet him. But the curtains parted and I saw the pale smear of a face framed in tousled hair and the woman's slightly startled eyes. I raised a finger to my mouth and with a nod of my head indicated that she should come outside. She nodded her head to say: Why? With a movement of my head I answered: Because. She shook her head and mouthed: No. The curtains drew closed and I leaned back against the wall of the house, lit a cigarette, and began to wait.

In the village the first roosters crowed tentatively.

The cigarette went out and I tried to strike a match so that the woman – if she was still on the couch – would hear and would know that I was waiting. The match cracked perfectly; the woman must have heard it.

The soil under the apple trees near the bathhouse hadn't been dug over, and it had been left unplanted so that there would be grass to feed the rabbits near at hand. Just there. And I was wearing a thick new down coat.

I reached for a second cigarette.

Under the apple trees by the bathhouse. In the mist.

The roosters sensed that dawn was breaking in the east and started calling out. The mist grew thicker. Someone passed by in the street; at first I only heard the footsteps, then I made out a dark figure, though of a man or a woman I couldn't tell. Probably a woman, a milkmaid.

Let them walk by – there's so much mist in the garden that no one could see a thing.

But then the mist suddenly took on colours and started thinning, dissipating; birds burst into song, dogs began to bark, buckets clanked at the well, a tractor started up somewhere nearby, and rays of sunlight fell on the village and hung in the garden among the dark and flower-speckled trees. The door creaked, the front steps creaked. I grew cold, peered from behind a corner of the house, and saw the old man, yawning, scratching himself, unshaven, heavy, in his undershirt and wide blue shorts.

*

Winters are terrible in the hot, dusty East. When I went into the army I thought I would be living in perpetual warmth. Of course there would be changes of seasons: scorching summer, hot autumn, and a soft winter of warm rains. And the first winter there wasn't much snow, it all melted during the day, and on the European new year it teemed with rain, not a warm rain, true, and cold mists rose on the steppes from morning until midday. But the second winter was harsh: snow, bitter cold, wind – it was best not to climb up onto the freezing armour-plating of a self-propelled gun without gloves. On operations we were issued felt-lined boots with rubber soles, insulated overtrousers, and a few trenchcoats per team that we would use to cover ourselves with at night in the self-propelled gun in the icy deserts or in the pale mountains under the stars. Our faces were blackened by the winter mountain sun and the freezing desert winds.

Our weatherproof tent was heated by two little stoves. It was warm when the stoves were running on heating fuel, but after a platoon in another regiment was burned to death in its tent we were forbidden to use the stuff anymore. They brought us coal, but not much, and for coal kindling wood was needed. Empty ammo boxes would do the trick, but then first one stool disappeared, then another, and soon the only things you could sit on in the tent were bunks. The officers tore a strip off us, but not harshly. The stoves didn't work well and in the morning our clothes and hair would have turned grey with frost. And when I was drying my leggings by the stove at night or lying under my two damp blankets and listening to the whistle of the wind off the steppes, I would start to think about the winters at The Belles.

In winter the house at The Belles would become the House. The garden was bare and black and choked with snowdrifts,

snowdrifts everywhere, and the fields glistened in the sunlight, and the only way one could get to the birch forest was on skis, and the river flowed soundlessly under solid ice and snow – as though there had never been a river there, as though its swimming holes and their yellow and white water-lilies, multi-coloured dragonflies, and singing frogs had been nothing more than a dream.

Wolves would howl in the fields at night.

The first to get up was the old man's wife. She would light the large burner in the stove and use the stove fork to put cast-iron pots of potatoes and beetroots on the flame; then she would go into the big room to light the firewood that had been drying overnight in the smaller, unpainted, tile-covered stove. If the temperature hadn't risen above thirty below during the night, the house would get cold: cross the naked floorboards barefoot and even the sweetest drowsiness vanished as if by magic. And there, in the stove's smaller chamber, the logs of birch and aspen started blazing and collapsing with a groan. All that could be seen from the couch was the stove's reflection in the enormous mirror over the brown cupboard; waking up, I watched the glowing, burning-hot rays crossing each other in the cold depth of the mirror. And in the darkness I saw the cheap icon with its kerchief and paper flowers, and the sleeping woman beside me.

Smoke was wafting gently from the stove, and with the smoke came heat as well, and soon the air in the house became bitter, hot, and damp, and one had to throw off one's bedclothes.

The copper pendulum of the heavy wooden clock on the wall was swaying back and forth. It was morning, but outside it was still pitch-black: the stars were shining, the plaster on the house was cracking, and occasional straining sounds reached up from the river. The ice was splitting in the cold.

But to leave the aromatic house for the nocturnal morning, to wash one's overheated face in the icy darkness, that was a joy. And afterwards to wait the whole incandescent day for the return to the house, with its stoves, soft felt boots, the anticipation of evening tea and long conversations with the old man. Comfortable, lazy winters.

And the voluptuousness of spring. And the June storms, the abundant roses of July, the blue of August. And the time of autumn labours and feasts, when the forest turns yellower and yellower with every passing day, the little maple on the church cupola is drowned in ochre, the rye and wheat are being harvested in the fields, the peasant women are bundling sheaves of flax, the days are very hot, the nights already cold, and shooting stars tumble, raising dust, from the vault of the heavens . . .

Standing on step-ladders and stools, the woman, the old man, and the old man's wife are picking apples from the branches, and I am lugging full willow baskets into the hall, carefully tipping them on their sides, and with a thud the apples spill out onto stretched-out old tablecloths. We have picked the apples in one day, the apple trees are empty and light, all except the Antonovkas, whose time has not yet come.

Preserves and jam are being made, golden juice is slowly streaming from the wooden press, and I am already sick of apples, and the woman is sick too. But she, it seems, not from the apples.

So, finished. For his labours the old man demands wine. I demand it too, but without speaking. The old man's wife fetches a clay jug from the cellar.

Now we break our backs for the potatoes. We go to the field armed with pitchforks. The old man and I dig them up; the women squat down and pick the lumpy tubers from the earth. Here a day is not enough. In the evening we will load the dry potatoes into sacks, carry them down into the basement, and empty them. At dinner I sit like a wooden statue. The women reward us with potatoes and creamed mushrooms and pancakes.

But then we have emptied the very last sack, and a little while later we have burned the leafy haulms – throughout the whole countryside, the whole land from the Baltics to the Urals, little wisps of aromatic smoke are rising.

The days are becoming shorter, the sun colder, the skies clearer. And the radio is threatening rain. The kitchen garden should be dug over for winter before the bad weather sets in. The old man says that we'll make it, but we don't, and under low drizzling grey clouds we are bent over, our clothes soaked with sweat and moisture, our faces warm and cold at the same time, the earth fills with weight and sticks to our shovels, and soon enough a real rain is beating against our oilskins and old felt caps.

But that's it. The house is ready for the siege: its belly is packed with potatoes, the larder has been stuffed with barrels of pickled cabbage, mushrooms, and cucumbers in brine, and the barrels reek of garlic, dill, and currant leaf; the shelves are crowded with jars of preserved fruit and jams; there are stacks of firewood under the lime trees, and on the wall behind the stove are bunches of dark red and golden onions; the storm windows have been put up, and between the panes are wadding and glossy scarlet pods of native pepper – looking at them makes one long for New Year's Eve. The hay loft is piled to overflowing.

'Well then,' the old man says, rubbing his calloused hands. 'Eh?'

His wife is content and without any extra talk she puts a jug on the table, then another. My woman hardly eats anything; her face is pale and her eyes sickly. The old man asks me:

'Have you been baptized?'

I answer no.

'That's bad,' the old man says. 'You should be, going off to the army. Soon there will be – ' the old man says ' – there will be someone else.' He looks at my woman. 'You and the newcomer – ' my woman blushes ' – will be baptized together. All right?'

In the evening I sit in the loft with a lamp in front of the black window, smoking Grodno cigarettes and writing long letters to friends and to the hermit philosopher who lives among pine trees and rock outcrops on the shores of Lake Baikal. Rain against the roof.

It rains and rains.

I walk up the softened path, a new willow basket on my back, through the garden. I pass through the gate, cross the potato field, open the barn door, fill the basket with hay, throw the cord across my shoulder, wind the end around my hand, haul the hay-filled basket towards the house, and look at my tracks: black smudges against white. Snow has fallen during the night.

I don't go in to the cow – she doesn't like me, threatens me with her horns, looks darkly at me. I call the old man, who pours the hay into her manger. The cow breathes and ruminates; she has long eyelashes and is called Marta; she is red.

The woman is a red-head too, and her breasts are heavy and her belly enormous. Time passes, and one day a nurseling appears, who screams, dribbles, burps milk, sleeps, wakes up, and suckles and suckles. There are nappies everywhere, rose-coloured nappies strung up across the wintry garden too. The woman lubricates her swollen nipples with grease so they won't chap. The nurseling suckles and suckles, dozes and suckles, and flies into a rage if a rubber dummy is slipped into its mouth instead of live, soft, warm flesh.

A young man, bearded, fresh, over-serious, arrives on a white crisp sunny Sunday. From his briefcase he pulls a vial of holy water, a brush, a cross, a book, a taper, and a cassock. The nurseling listens attentively to Father Alexander, looks at the flame on the taper, and shoves its hand in its mouth.

After having read the appropriate prayers and sprinkled me and the baby with holy water, Father Alexander smiles shyly and puts the cross on the baby, and then on me.

The baptism ends with a meal. The old man insists: A little vodka, Father Alexander, a little vodka; Father Alexander says no, no, but he presses him and Father Alexander takes a little sip. On the other hand he eats well and gladly accepts the old man's tea . . .

I dream of the old man and Father Alexander, and I dream of the red-coloured Marta chasing the chubby naked nurseling around the garden, she catches him, rolls over on her side and exposes her udder like a dog, closes her eyes . . . In the weatherproof tent, in a self-propelled gun amid pale icy mountains, in the shadow of reddish rocks, I dreamed of a low hill and a row of spruce. The days went by, it was the seven-hundredth day, and more and more days, and finally I dreamed my last dream of The Belles.

Speckled helicopters were flying around in the sky, the tank treads were crunching, and from time to time a spurt of smoke, sand, metal, and shreds of leather, clothing, and rubber would rise up into the air; a helicopter would land and soldiers would run towards it dragging a tarpaulin. We were creeping into a mountain range that stretched towards Pakistan, and over and over again we would come to a halt and dig trenches. The earth would drum under our pickaxes and shovels, with the sun scorching, flies clouding, tight red blisters bursting in our palms. Once the guns were in place we would open fire into the mountains and inhale dust and gunpowder. Before morning came we would strip everything down and move somewhere else. Helicopters were continually evacuating soldiers with torn pants and wet, sticky shirts. Two years of life on the steppes and in the mountains lay behind us. We seemed to have been forgotten; we wandered through the ravines and plateaux gouging out trenches, drinking raw water from canals and streams, sluicing the rocks with our diarrhoea.

We were sitting around smoking and watching a turtle. The sergeant was tapping it with a hammer. He was hitting it harder and harder . . . Suddenly the battalion commander ran up and shouted: Pack it up, battery! Back to camp! And the sergeant swung, struck, and the turtle's armour burst and spattered our boots.

Darkness fell. We were ready, the second battery was ready, as were the infantry battalion, the tank crews, and the mortar batteries – everyone was ready, everyone was waiting. Plump stars hung over the mountain peaks, and then the start commands rang out, and engines roared to life, the column shook, creaked, and ground stones under its treads.

No one slept. The column was running with its lights out. The peaks stood black and massive, and the column slowly wound its way through rocky pads, under granite faces, the length of long, tense tails.

For two or three hours the column headed towards the mountains.

Day broke.

I was sitting behind the heavy machine-gun, leaning against the top of a hatch, staring at the now-colourless stars, at the greyish crags and peaks, staring in a daze, eyes wide, shaking my head, mouth open, and the stars were bursting like blisters, a crowbar struck the armour of a gigantic turtle, the blisters burst, and suddenly a breach lit up. I squeezed through with difficulty, getting myself dirty, and the old man saw me on the white road and ran, barefoot through the snow, past the lime trees, past the well, along the spruce, and vanished into the church; he ran into the church, and in its empty windows a copper light flared up, and a pealing of bells illuminated the peasant huts and my muddy face; I trembled, stooped over, sank down, and fell to my knees in the snowy earth.

The Snow-Covered House

It was autumn, and mists enveloped the garden in the morning, it rained, the birds were silent. People, the trees, the dogs, and the mute birds were waiting – the first snow was due to fall any day. And a woman was waiting for a man.

The woman lived in an orange-roofed wooden house surrounded by a bare, gnarled, fluttering garden. The house with the orange roof stood among other wooden and brick single-storey houses on the outskirts of a city of steel and concrete. From a window in the house one could see the onion of the old church of Saint John Chrysostom, which, framed by the black branches of the lime tree, was a pleasant sight. But she only rarely and by chance looked out through this window; more often, and more purposefully, she would sit by the opposite window, the south-east window. From this window one could watch the street down which the man would be coming home from the war in the East.

The house had two rooms, with green wallpaper, a kitchen, and a white stove. On a wall in the hallway hung a reproduction of Van Gogh's 'Red Vineyards' – women were picking grapes amid crimson shrubs, a man was walking down a road as translucent as a river, and behind him the sun was burning low over the earth. The painting – those terrible crimson smears and that black silhouette on the road – frightened the woman. The woman would try not to look at the painting, but the painting compelled her to look at it and when she did her arms and legs turned to cotton wool. She would have been happy to take it down and hide it away somewhere, but it was the man's favourite painting and for some reason she was afraid to remove it. Nor – for two years – had she washed the shirt the man used to wear before the war. All in all she had become superstitious in the last couple of years. She would think to herself, I'm superstitious, a silly fool, and smile wryly, but she prayed anyway. At school she led the children in discussions about atheism, but at home, staring off to the east, she would whisper a prayer she had made up herself: 'God-God-God, beloved and dear, gentle and tender, I love you and I implore you, God-God-God.' She couldn't imagine what would happen if a student or a fellow-teacher overheard her prayer. When she thought about it she went pale and broke out in scarlet spots. She knew that there was no God, that there were all sorts of chemical processes, evolution, and a few strange things that science hadn't explained yet, although eventually it would. And she was sure that no one, no benevolent God, heard her prayer, that her prayer wouldn't save her man at war in the East – while she was whispering by the south-east window the telegram had already arrived at the war registry, they had already sent her a notice to come to the war registry so they could solemnly inform her: 'Your husband . . .' They had already loaded the metallic box into an aeroplane, and the aeroplane was already droning in the skies over Russia. She understood everything clearly. But once she had woken up and whispered through her tears: 'God-God-God, I love you and implore you.' And from then on it had become a habit.

A short letter had come. The man had written that this would be his last letter – soon a helicopter would fly into camp and take them away. Just now the weather was too bad for flying, but soon.

It was late in the autumn and the icy mists smelled of snow.

The woman would wake up very early. She would get up early to do her hair. After her bath and breakfast she would sit down in front of her mirror, her tubes, little boxes, combs, and perfume bottles laid out on her little table, and start to primp and arrange her light-coloured hair, which was neither very thick nor very long. The scruffy grey cat would stretch, come over to her, arch its tail, and purr deeply while rubbing itself against her legs, and the feel of its fur against her legs would raise goosepimples.

She usually gathered her hair in a bun at the back and fastened it with a rubber band, but recently she had been going off to school with intricate crowns and waves on her head, and the male teachers were saying about her 'Aha' and taking a second look, and they realized that she was very young, that her cheeks were white, her lips the colour of roses, that she had beautiful calves and arms, and when she walked . . . It was best not to look at her too long from behind when she walked. And they remembered that her husband was serving in the army some-where.

She had been an ordinary young woman, like hundreds and thousands of others, but when her man was due to come home she suddenly changed and the bald Boris Savelyevich, the Russian teacher, stared after her in astonishment, his mouth went dry, and wild thoughts rushed through his head like heavy freight trains. And the athletics instructor, a man of deeds and not dreams, flirted with her during break and asked if he couldn't come and split her wood pile for her. And yes, the boys of course goggled their eyes at her, mechanically tugging on their sparse little moustaches, picking at the pimples on their foreheads, and drawing in their imaginations pictures no less wild than the fantasies of Boris Savelyevich.

The women at the school were shocked and mortified. The athletics instructor, the Russian teacher, the groundsman, the drill instructor – all had stopped paying attention to them and, as though in the grip of some powerful elixir, were now casting voluptuous looks at the woman and making half-pleasant, half-ribald *double-entendres* to her. But what had happened? Nothing at all. Nothing new in her clothes, no lipstick, no shadow on her eyelashes: everything was the way it had been before, only the hairstyle was different.

For her part, the headmistress had immediately formulated an explanation for the change that had occurred: a graphic expression of sexuality. That was bad – it was a pernicious influence on the moral atmosphere. Some measures had to be taken – but which measures? The graphic expression of sexuality was not prohibited by a single paragraph in the regulations. The headmistress examined her subordinate carefully but could find no breach of regulations anywhere: skirt sufficiently chaste, blouse opaque, no excessive make-up. Hairstyle? The headmistress had the same one, crowns and waves too, everyone had crowns and waves and curls, so that it was in fact her former hairstyle, a simple ponytail, that had ben provocative, while this one had simply joined the general chorus of hairstyles. Absolutely nothing out of the ordinary here . . . but good lord, the way she flashes her eyes around like that – sexual, dangerously explosive!

The woman waiting for her man to come home from the East did not notice the cold scorn of the ladies at school, nor the rapture of the pimpled adolescents, nor the attentions of the scholastic knights – the muscular athletics instructor, the dry, wrinkled drill instructor, the bald, dreamy Boris Savelyevich, the fat, grey-haired groundsman with the false left eye. She was waiting.

When she came home from school she lit the stove, heated two pails of water and used the warm water to wash the floors, wiped the furniture down with a damp cloth, and continued cleaning and scrubbing things even though the house had been sparkling for a long time now. The cat wandered after her from room to room, watching all these preparations with an air of sarcasm. In fact he looked at everything sceptically: he had intelligent eyes, his bushy light pelt bristled on his jowls like muttonchops, and he was content, sluggish, fluffy.

The woman tried not to raise her eyes to 'Red Vineyards', and she succeeded for some time, but in the end her eyes were pulled to the painting. She stared at it fixedly and told herself: what of it then? Autumn, red leaves on the vines, women collecting bunches of grapes into baskets, the sun hanging in the distance, and a common tramp is marching down the road that flows like a river, he's a vagrant – the people are working and he's walking along, his hands thrust in his pockets, whistling, no doubt, and it's obvious that he has neither a home nor a family, and he has no idea where the road is leading: that's all. And, to be honest, it was unfathomable what the man saw in this crap. A crazy artist had put – no, had thrown – paint on a canvas, and now everyone says, 'Oh! Oh! Oh!' The first thing I'll do when he comes back is say I don't like this piece of crap, oh God, I'll tell him . . . God-God-God, beloved and great, good, gentle, I love you and pray to you . . .

But no, not at first, at first I didn't hate this stupid painting at all, before that I had been indifferent to it, but then one autumn he wrote a letter in which he mentioned crimson grape leaves behind a shattered, shell-pocked *duval*, and – so . . . And that tramp isn't a tramp but a messenger, and he knows where he's going . . . What nonsense!

Later she took the second pail off the stove, fastened the door on its hook, drew the blinds, and took a bath in a large basin. After her bath she dried herself with a long, thick, soft towel and moved from the kitchen into the bedroom, where she stopped in front of the big mirror in the corner. She looked at herself from every side, slapped her taut, still-childless stomach, and tried to see herself through the eyes of the man, who was no longer fighting the war in the East but sitting and waiting for the weather to clear so he could fly home in an aeroplane. He was sitting there in the East, in some weather-proofed tent with a makeshift stove, sitting there with all his sunburned, broad-shouldered, dour friends, smoking a cigarette, not saying anything, or maybe talking in his deep, slow voice . . . Telling them that he had a house with an orange roof, a stove, a cat, and a wife . . .

After eating she would sit in the south-east window correcting exercise books and preparing for the next day's lessons. She would sit with her head hunched over the table and hear, or rather sense, someone walking down the street; not moving, holding her breath, she would raise her long eyes with their short pale lashes to the window and look outside. Someone would in fact be walking down the street: a woman carrying bags, the old neighbour in his tattered winter hat, a yoke slung over his shoulder, a little boy, a drunk, a flashily dressed young woman, or just a mongrel ranging around on its pressing dog business. The garden was black and bare, and rivulets of rain were coursing down the rough torsos of the apple and plum trees. Rain-rain, splish-splash-plosh-plash-plish — but the ground was already soaked through and couldn't absorb the water from the skies, and there was water in every dip and cranny, flowing in streams towards the river. Rain-rain, splish-splash, plish-plash, plish-plash . . .

The cat was dozing on the sofa while it rained. Everything was all right with him, he didn't remember the man now fighting the war in the East, he wasn't waiting for anyone.

But of course he's not fighting now, no, not fighting, the woman thought, forgetting about the exercise books and tomorrow's classes, no, not fighting but sitting in his tent, and against the tent splish-splash-rain. And thinking of me and of the distant view from the roof, the prominent roof – before the war he had stained it himself in that orange colour, the best in the world, the colour of good luck. God! If you grant me my wish I promise never again to tell the schoolchildren that you don't exist – I can leave the school so that I'll never tell anyone you don't exist, I can go to church every day to listen to the priests sing, to light candles in front of the icons – just make it so that he comes back, I beg you.

Towards evening her ears were aching with the song of the rain, her eyes loathing the street and the passers-by. She fed the cat and let it out into the street, then made a supper of tea and biscuits – she couldn't eat anything more – and after supper she bolted the door, turned out the light, undressed, and climbed into bed. She lay there breathing softly and listening. For a long time she couldn't fall asleep. She lay there and listened intently. It was awful, and her feet were freezing. The house was warm but her feet were freezing. Since the man had left for the East her feet would freeze in bed. And it felt as though the house was in the middle of a forest and that someone was roaming around it, rapping his nails against the windows and scratching at the door.

Are there really women who live their whole lives without a man, she asked herself. It's awful to be alone, and your feet feel cold in bed.

The Chinese say . . . What was I thinking about? Oh, yes, yes, she remembered, about the dead boy lying with open eyes in a dark room.

A year before she had left her house in the morning and had seen a person in the ditch near the house next door; it was a fair-haired teenager with thin shoulders, long legs, and his jacket in the mud.

The world was always threatening; as soon as she had begun to understand things she perceived that, and later she knew it. The world was threatening even when the man was around – absolutely. But he had hard shoulders, strong fists, a peaceful air, and a low, confident voice. He stood between her and the world. But then they had sent him to the East, and the world had drawn inward and pressed in on her.

But the Chinese . . . the Chinese what? But the Chinese say: yin and yang, everything that exists – yin and yang, the feminine principle and the masculine. Yang is everything powerful, bright, solar. Yin is everything weak, dim, lunar. Lord, how true. And to sleep alone, so cold, is really like having moonlight and not blood flowing inside you . . . God-God! Bring me back my yang!

A week and a half had passed since his last letter. The woman cleaned her nest every day, and every morning decorated her hair with crowns and curls, and the school Don Juans continued to run after her like rats enchanted by the Pied Piper's flute. And very soon the snow would begin; the people, the dogs, the trees, and the birds were all waiting for it. And the woman in the house with the orange roof was waiting for her man. She was yin, and at night her feet were as cold as ice.

And at last, on Monday, early in the morning, flakes, shreds, and wisps began to fly, and the earth parted from the black sky and dimly started glowing. Snow.

The Snow-Covered House

The woman didn't have classes that day, but she got up early and saw that the sky had become unglued from the earth. She threw on a man's sheepskin coat and went out onto the doorstep. The cat, who had spent the night tooling around somewhere, sang a short hoarse song and darted into the house. The snow was falling in lumps. The lumps were flying and flying down, hanging from the branches of the apple and plum trees, plopping into puddles, sticking to the orange roof, paving the matted, heavy road, rounding off and softening the roofs and chimneys, trees, flowerbeds, stacks of firewood. The woman's heart suddenly stood still, her breathing faltered, and for a moment she sensed a terrible lightness, as though she would break away from the doorstep and soar around in the sky. It passed immediately. Her face burning, the woman went back into the house. She realized that it would be today.

The cat mewed stridently – me! meow! me! – and the woman fed it. She didn't want to eat anything; she drank cold tea and chewed a sweet. A flame was already rising in the stove and pots of water stood on the burners. The woman turned on all the lights and carefully examined the room. She made the bed and heaped her notepads and books in a pile on the table. She washed the floor. Her face was blazing, her heart beating heavily, painfully, and her head was spinning.

'What's the matter with me?' the woman asked out loud, and thought: What's the matter with me? Not today, perhaps, what am I . . . tomorrow, perhaps . . . or in two days, three, four.

But her face was on fire, her heart was thumping as though she'd been running for miles, and from time to time her head froze and turned numb. In the street the snow was falling, coarse and white. The flame was fluttering in the stove . . . fluttering somehow playfully, not like usual, and even the tramp in the Van Gogh painting was walking more joyfully down the liquid, translucent road, and those huge-rumped women were more cheerfully plucking clusters of grapes off the vine and putting them in large baskets. The woman took a bath and scented herself with a green-coloured perfume, put on a dress, and did her hair.

It was slowly getting lighter. Too slowly. The woman had no idea what to do now. Everything was ready; the house with the orange roof was waiting for its master from the East – the doorstep was waiting, the stove was waiting, the rooms were waiting, and the French wine-growers were hurrying to gather every cluster before his arrival.

Day broke. The snow was still falling. The earth was white and soft, the roofs were soft and white, as were the apple and plum branches and the rounded hills and tiny little houses and small gardens beyond the river, and the cupola of the church of Saint John Chrysostom, but the fences and walls stuck out a mournful black.

The woman wandered around the house, bent down, absent-mindedly stroked the cat. She took a book down off the shelf, leafed through it, read a few sentences without understanding them, slammed it shut, and replaced it in the rows of books. The clock showed ten. Snow was still flying outside the windows.

Should she bake some blinis? No, the blinis would get cold, and they're not as good re-heated. Should she put some lipstick on? But he didn't like it when she wore lipstick. But suppose he liked it now? But what if he didn't? The woman put some lipstick on in front of the mirror. She smiled. No, too bright. She rubbed her lips lightly with cotton wool. Now there was almost nothing.

It was snowing outside the windows.

For some reason it seemed to her that he wouldn't come just now. He wouldn't come at eleven, he wouldn't come at twelve.

He would come in three hours, or six, but it couldn't be just now – it would be impossible for him to show up so early.

At twelve the snow slackened, and the air gradually lightened and became clear and frosty, although the sky was not blue but in fact had remained grey. The world was fresh and plump . . .

The woman smiled: she had thought of some work to do. She threw off her dress, put on some woollen trousers, a sweater, and a knitted ski cap, grabbed some gloves, put on her boots, and went out into the street. Squinting from the whiteness, she ploughed through the snow to the toolshed, opened the door, and brought out a wooden shovel.

She was clearing the pathway. The snow was light, but a lot of it had fallen and the woman was growing breathless and flushed. She was sweeping the pathway of snow and thinking: There, a white holiday. She was also thinking: It would be nice if he were here this minute, when my cheeks are rosy, I feel fresh, and he will find me all fresh in the middle of this fresh garden. It's just too bad that snow is pasted all over the orange roof.

But neither at that moment nor in the others she spent in the garden with the shovel did he arrive.

After clearing off the whole path the woman reluctantly headed into the house. At the doorstep she stopped, turned around, and inspected the garden . . . A blue-grey bird was sitting in the far apple tree. A few tiny, black, rotten, wrinkled apples were hanging on the far apple tree and the bird flew up to pick at them. The woman stood motionless. The bird looked like a pigeon, only more graceful. The woman was watching the smoke-coloured bird and trying to remember what it was called. The forest visitor twirled its head, stuck out its neck, and pecked at the black fruit, then immediately started nervously looking around. Nothing terrible happened, nothing was creeping towards it through the garden, and the bird was already boldly nipping at the apple, and again, and again. Then a second bird silently appeared, perched on the very same tree, and then the first let out a guttural, throaty sound and the woman remembered what the birds were called: turtle doves. And again the woman's head began to spin and her body turned weightless. Today. And perhaps now.

It was two in the afternoon. The birds had left the garden and the garden was empty. Every now and then people went by in the street: men, women, children, old people – all of them alien and hateful.

When evening set in the woman fried yesterday's potatoes on the electric burner and heated some tea. She couldn't even eat the potatoes: she tasted them and covered the pan with a lid. She drank a cup of tea and ate a bit of buttered white bread. Neither at seven at night, nor at ten at night, nor at one in the morning did the doorstep creak under the man's weight. The woman turned out the light, undressed, and lay down. She had kept her woollen socks on so that her feet wouldn't freeze, but her feet froze even in the thick woollen socks, her face was freezing, and rare warm drops were sliding down her cold face.

In the morning she woke up and sensed a sort of dry clarity in her soul, and she thought: not today. And her dreams, such an odd kind of dream, had also said: not today. But she did her hair. She ate breakfast and fed the cat.

Then, while she was gathering her notebooks, she saw through the window that the postwoman, in a sweater and shawl and with a satchel at her side, was walking along the fence. The postwoman went as far as the gate, thrust newspapers and one envelope into the flat metal box, and walked off unhurriedly down the liquid and muddy road.

The mail just brought the latest newspapers, the woman thought slowly. And in the envelope is just a letter from some girlfriend, she thought slowly, staring, in a daze, out of the window at the blue mailbox.

She stood up. She crossed the doorstep and walked down the path through a cold mist towards the mailbox that hung on the gate's dark crosses.

Someone simply sent a letter. That's all. That's all there is to it, she thought drunkenly.

She drew the newspapers and the letter out of the box.

The now-grey flesh on her face broke out into wrinkles, a vein protruded on her temple, dark semicircles had spread under her eyes – and with a simian face the woman unsealed the envelope.

A Springtime Walk

Soft country roads were carrying them up onto hilltops, leading them down into damp depressions, and the sky was now coming nearer, now casting precipitously upwards, a sky of rare clouds and larks beating their wings.

The young man in his threadbare, greasy cloth cap was riding slightly ahead; he was the guide, he'd been riding or walking these roads for several years, he knew their every twist and turn, every tree and hill along the way. He was cranking the pedals and now and again looking over his shoulder at his companion.

The soft roads were bearing them through green hills, green fields, the clouds were standing still in the sky and the sun was shining yellow. He looked at her over his shoulder, stretched his thick lips, and she smiled in response. He was thinking: it's wonderful, of course, that she's coming too, that at last she's seeing these places, it's wonderful, but it would be better if he were alone. He was used to being alone. At first it had been overwhelming, especially at night – a bird would screech, a branch fall, footsteps rustle – but then his fear had vanished. And one day he became sure that he was better off alone: he had blabbed about the Coffee Ponds to a classmate, who had asked to come along, and everything had turned out awfully – the

classmate had talked and talked, laughed loudly, greedily hauled
carp out of the water, tried to hit a duck with a rock, cut down
live aspen for no reason and more than once had said that there
was nothing to be afraid of in a forest, a forest is just a stack of
trees . . . and everything was awful, everything was wrong. Of
course she wasn't the classmate. But still.

They crossed the train tracks – oil-soaked ties, the crunch of
the embankment, the black caps of the railway spikes, and the
narrow, shiny tracks running off into the distance – and he
thought: yes, soon. The soft country road picked them up again,
and again they were emerging over the brows of hills and going
down into damp, fetid defiles.

Yes, soon, he was thinking. In three days. That's all. Then two
years of it. Boots, barracks. But that was nonsense – two years
wasn't twenty-five years, the way it had been in the old days.

And he started wondering if it had been right to bring her with
him. What could they see in one day? To go everywhere – to the
pines, to the red stream, to Fox Hill, to the ponds, the village –
would take more than a day. But because of her they had to be
back in the city today. Her parents knew nothing, they were sure
that their daughter had walked to the institute in the morning
and that from lunch until evening she would be taking notes in
the reading room at the institute library. But in her case along
with her schoolbooks and notepads she had put plimsolls,
trousers, a tee-shirt, bread, and sausage, and she had come to
him, changed, and there she was, riding next to him down the
soft road on a bicycle he had borrowed from a friend, laboriously
cranking its pedals, not asking to stop, although she wasn't used
to it and was already getting tired, smiling whenever he glanced
back at her. And her tee-shirt was already damp. It was morning,
but the sun was hot. May.

The travelled road forked away, but they kept going straight on. They rode down an overgrown, unstable road that soon led into a swamp.

She dutifully took her plimsolls off when he did, rolled her trousers up to her knees, and gingerly sank her white feet into the cold and oily mire.

'Are there snakes here?' she asked, breathing heavily.

He was walking in front. He looked back and said, 'Snakes? I've been coming here for three years . . . In three years I – not once . . .' And he fell silent; he had spotted a brownish-green rubber pretzel off to his left. A small young snake was lying motionless on the dry, sunny, hummock. One would have thought it was dead, but its eyes were moist and two dots of sunlight were shining in them.

He took his eyes off the hummock and calmly said, 'No. These are blessed places, I swear.'

They were steaming hot, bathed in sweat, mosquitoes were landing on them, and they were slapping their faces, twitching their shoulders, and racing to make it across the swamp. The mire bubbled, sucked, and gurgled under their feet. The mud was cold, the air warm, the sun burned the clothes on their backs and shoulders.

Just like that, he was thinking, not one snake in three years, but today, on this last day . . . He turned round, cast a glance at his companion's legs . . . She looked at him quizzically and put on an expression of cheerfulness. Her face was wet, red, stained with bloody smudges; there was a dark crushed mosquito on her cheek.

'We'll be out of this soon,' he said.

He should have come here alone. And now he was afraid that she would be bitten by a snake.

They made it across the swamp, walked for a while over hard ground through thickets of willow, and found themselves in a clearing under a hillside. The clearing was yellow with flowering dandelions. Bees and bumblebees were toiling away, glassy wings were flashing everywhere over the flowers, and they could hear a quiet velvet humming. A white clay eye was visible over where the clearing met the hillside and started rising smoothly. A spring was pulsating and circles were spreading out on its translucent surface.

'This is it, isn't it? The Bedouin God?' The young woman dropped her bicycle and walked to the spring. She bent down over the roiling water, froze, and glanced back helplessly at him. He came over and looked into the spring. On its slimy white bottom, slowly rotating as though performing a lazy dance, was a dead frog. He rolled up his sleeves, plunged his arm up to the elbow in the water, pulled out the frog, and tossed it into the flowers.

'Once,' he said, wiping his hand on his trousers, 'I found a grey bird with an eye torn out in this spring. A hawk or a harrier must have just missed it.'

'The Bloodthirsty God,' she answered, staring at the spring in disgust.

He shrugged his shoulders and leaned down over the water. After drinking some he looked, mockingly, at his companion. She pursed her lips and turned away.

'Drink – what's the matter with you?'

'Nothing. You didn't have to tell me about that bird.'

'It was a long time ago., Drink.'

Her mouth was as hot and dry as the land of those Bedouin with their camels. He'd made that up himself – the God of the Bedouin. She smiled.

'Drink,' he repeated.

'Drink, drink,' she mimicked, then frowned, bent her head down, and stretched her lips out to the longed-for water.

Afterwards she looked at her feet, wiggled her muddy toes, and said, 'I should wash myself off.'

He pulled a small cup out of his backpack, scooped water from the spring, and poured it over her feet. She rubbed her feet and gasped from the cold. Then she quickly put on her socks and shoes and jumped around on the spot to warm up. Her bangs were hitting her forehead and her breasts were jiggling under her tee-shirt.

He took his eyes off her, lay down in the grass, and said, 'Let's rest.'

She sat down a little way off.

The bumblebees were buzzing.

'But doesn't this place have a name? The stream is the God of the Bedouin, of course, but the clearing?'

He answered that it wasn't called anything.

'But I would have had to christen this clearing something. It's so nice.'

'What would you have christened it?' he asked reluctantly.

'Anything . . . whatever comes into your head.' She wrinkled her brows. 'Bumblebee Meadow. Hmm?'

He was looking at the sky through his eyelashes and said nothing.

'Isn't that good?' she asked.

'They're everywhere here.'

She didn't understand. 'What?'

'Meadows. There are lots of flowery clearings around here.'

'Fine, if you want to be like that, be like that,' she said, turning away.

She felt hurt. He had to say something, but the sun was burning his flesh through his shirt and his tongue was thick, and his eyelids were heavy, and he didn't want to think about anything, he didn't want anything. He was lying back, silent. She was sitting and watching the striped bumblebees. The bumble-bees were settling down on the dandelions gathering nectar, and roving through their stamens as though through a soft yellow forest.

Two sparkling points, brownish-green rubber pretzel, you didn't have to be here today, on this last day, and now I have to worry about you biting the girl. The snake raised its head slightly and smiled a thin smile. He shuddered, opened his eyes, and remembered that the girl was probably feeling hurt. He sat up and said, 'Yes, that's it, it's fine, fine.'

'What?' she asked in an indifferent voice, tightening her eyes. She wasn't looking at him, but her eyes were narrow with aloofness and disdain.

'Come on, Bumblebee Meadow.'

'Ah,' she responded. 'Thanks for the favour.'

He burst out laughing and the girl looked at him severely. He stopped laughing.

'Sorry, but it's funny,' he muttered. 'What are we arguing for?'

'I have no intention of arguing. As far as I can tell we have nothing to argue about. And anyway I can . . . I know the way now.'

She knows that I'm wondering if it had been right to bring her along on this last walk. I could have refused to but I didn't, I wanted her to come, didn't I? So why am I being an idiot?

'Oh, come on, let's not squabble, why are we, really, are we going to . . . what for? I just haven't had enough sleep, that's all. I feel a bit tired . . .'

'So sleep. I won't disturb you.'

'I don't want to any more. I'm ready for anything. Shall we get going? You feel rested? You're not tired, are you?' he asked her solicitously, looking her in the eyes. 'Do you want some more water? Shall I bring you some? Let me get you some.' He stood up, went to the stream, and brought back a cup of water. 'Drink. It's good water. I've never had better. Have you?'

The young girl couldn't restrain herself and burst out laughing, snorting into the cup and spraying his face.

They left the hollow and came out onto a knoll blooming with golden, long-stemmed flowers. She asked what the flowers were, somehow they were very familiar to her but she couldn't remember . . . He didn't manage to answer; the young girl spotted something on the meadow and cried out.

Out of the copse onto the meadow – it hadn't been mowed for years and years, it was overgrown, thick wild carrots, branching like pine trees, and absinthe bushes had shot up in it – came a horse. It was stocky, brown, with bulging flanks, a tangled mane, thick legs. The horse bowed its massive head, tore up some grass, and slowly chewed while casting its eyes around. At last it spotted the human beings. The horse stopped chewing and, pricking its ears and flaring its nostrils, stared at the two figures in the midst of the golden flowers. Realizing that they weren't elks, but humans, it snorted, bared its teeth, whinnied angrily, swung around, and trotted quickly back into the birches.

'It ran away,' the girl whispered. 'But where did it come from?'

'I don't know, maybe it escaped,' he replied in a whisper, then coughed and added, out loud, 'It's run off from a village. It didn't like something and it ran away. Maybe it didn't like pulling a cart, and ran off.'

'You said there wasn't a populated village around here.'

'From some village miles away. Wasn't it great?'

'Yes!'

'But there are loads of elk around here. And wild boar. One chased me once.'

'A wild boar?'

'Yes. It was with its family. I walked straight into them and it charged me, and there were only bushes around, not a single tree. But apparently it wasn't angry. It just chased me away and returned to the others.'

'I can imagine you running.'

'I ran fast. I knew it wasn't chasing me any more but I kept running anyway. After that I bought a gun. From this dealer.'

'So where is it?'

'Bah.' He waved his hand, threw his leg over his bicycle, sat on the saddle, and looked impatiently away.

The young woman was thinking how peaceful and nice it would be with a gun and asked him again where it was. He answered that he'd lost it, and she asked him where. He nodded his head off to the side: somewhere, over there somewhere.

They were riding down the brambled road. A bird flew high in the sky. In the swamp, among the intertwined willow branches, the horse was standing motionless.

A bird was soaring high in the sky. It was an old brown bird of prey with a mottled, light-coloured breast. It was describing circles in the thick blue between the clouds. Far below, grey, yellow, and golden patches were revolving slowly, puddles flashing out. Air currents were ruffling its feathers and washing over its hook-billed grey head. Below was the iridescent watery earth where birds and frogs were calling, bees and mosquitoes droning, where everything was restless and hot. The old bird was floating in the blue between the clouds, where everything was quiet and cool.

The horse was hiding in the bushes at the edge of the swamp. Mosquitoes and horseflies were flitting over the warm mountain of thick, sweaty flesh, and, with wings vibrating, were searching for tender spots, plunging their probosci into its flesh, sucking its blood. Flies swarmed over the suppurating wounds on its rump; the wounds were symmetrical, round, and deep. The horse stood among the bushes, narrowing its big brown eyes off to one side, pricking its ears to the sounds of the stifling spring day, striking at the blood-engorged suckers with its tail, shivering from the memory of the humans among the yellow flowers.

Deep in a swampy thicket, in the warm brown ruts between the hummocks, a herd of elk was sleeping lightly. Badgers and foxes with their cubs were dozing in their burrows on Fox Hill.

They rode through the meadow gone wild and looked at Fox Hill, tall and overgrown with shrubs. It jutted out over the stands of trees, a huge white patch on its side.

They crossed the meadow, made it over a depression that rolled into a field by pushing their bicycles beside them, climbed onto their bicycles again, and soon reached the hill. At the base of the hill they dismounted and clambered up through the grass and flowers.

The flowertips knocked against their ankles. Buzzing angrily, startled bees and bumblebees would rise up from the flowers, hover around their faces, and then reluctantly fly away.

A midday wind picked up.

The leaves on the bushes were fluttering, and the flowers and weeds tumbled over and stood up again. The wind was drying their sweaty faces and cooling their damp clothes. The girl's short dark hair was whipping and lashing against her forehead and cheeks.

They climbed to the summit of the hill. The girl looked around.

Below them green lagoons were boiling, and winy, violet, and lime dots and smudges glimmered. Larks were darting around in the translucent thickness of the blue sky, islands of willow and birch were floating off towards the horizon, and in the distance hung emerald hills and dark forests of pine.

A wild cherry bush was in bloom on the hill's western slope, a strong wind was blowing, and the aroma of wild cherry was barely perceptible on the summit of Fox Hill.

He took off his cloth cap, held his close-cropped knobbly head into the wind, and told her that he sometimes spent the night here. The girl remained silent. He didn't say anything more, and they stood, silent, looking around from the heights of the soft, green Fox Hill.

They climbed back down and he asked where she wanted to go next: to Red Stream, to the Coffee Ponds, or to the Village? But only one of them. It was already three o'clock and they'd be getting back late no matter what. At Red Stream they'd be able to swim and sunbathe. There were cranes living on the Coffee Ponds now, and she'd never seen a live crane before. But in the Village – he was telling her about the Village: oh, the Village! It was joy, pure and simple. To the Village, she said.

The Village stood near an old birch wood. First they spotted the long, thick birches, and after they had climbed a small hill was the Village.

The Village was in blossom. The gnarled cherry trees were in bloom, the apple trees, the lilac bushes. Around the huts and in the vegetable gardens were the dull yellowish coronas of dark henbane, the fluttering of egg-white dandelions, rosy meadowsweet, golden, pyramidal strands of flax. Purple honeysuckle cups were hanging among the stinging nettles, and their first flowers were extending their pale lips. Spreading hawthorn bushes were in bloom near the mossy, mould-covered well. Starlings and thrushes were chirruping, grey forest birds were trilling, chirping, whistling, flitting from branch to branch and littering the ground with white petals. Green moss covered the beams of the empty-windowed *izbas*, on whose rotted, collapsing roofs slender aspens, birches, and camomiles were sprouting. Everything smelled of flowers, greenery, rot, and mould.

'And I've fixed up a bathhouse. That's my hut over there.' He looked at her expectantly. 'Like it?'

'Here?' she asked, dismayed, and looked around.

'Yes. Only . . .'

'What?'

'Only that . . . it's just strange. Is it the well that smells like that?'

'Yes. I get water from a stream. There's a stream in the woods.'

They walked down the short village street between grey tumbledown *izbas*, past vegetable patches and gardens with dilapidated fences sticking up here and there from the green undergrowth.

A twisted bough hung above the door of the bathhouse hut.

'That's The Guardian,' he said, and then the girl made out a crooked mouth, a few thick hairs, and an empty eye in its forehead.

The door creaked and they entered the hut. Once she was used to the dark she could see a stove, an iron bed with a torn, straw-packed mattress, a table, a little glass-paned window, and just below the ceiling a shelf with a pile of candles, some matches, a packet of salt, a kettle, a cup and spoon, a pot. Everything smelled of must and stale smoke.

'It's so odd,' she murmured.

'We'll make dinner outside,' he said, and took the kettle and pot from the shelf.

He headed off towards the stream. The girl sat down and immediately felt worn out, exhausted. She didn't want to eat, but to lie down and stretch out her heavy, swollen feet . . . She lay back and fell into a doze.

When she went out he was already building a fire. He struck a match and lit the kindling; the flame licked the dry twigs and a moment later burst up and started to flicker against the bottom of the kettle and the water-filled pot.

'Do you come here in the winter too?' she asked, squatting down in front of the fire.

He nodded.

'It's odd here,' she said. 'Nice, but odd somehow. How did you find all this?'

'I was riding around looking for mushrooms and came across the ponds. Probably carp there, I thought . . . I came back with my fishing gear. There were carp, right enough. And there you are.'

'But how did you lose the gun? It doesn't feel right without a gun. Wolves and everything. And people could . . . Some fugitive. Do people come here often?'

'No, the swamp keeps them away. But sometimes a fisherman might . . . And in the winter hunters on skis come after rabbits.'

'The winter, yes, that must be great. A blizzard, wolves, and you stoking a fire.'

The water in the pot came to the boil. He wanted to toss in the groats but the girl asked if she could do it all, and he handed her the salt, the spoon with wire around its handle, the bag of groats, and the can of stewed meat. She poured three handfuls of groats and a pinch of salt into the boiling water and, her face turned away from the hot embers, began to stir the mixture with the wire-handled spoon. He was sitting across from her, looking at the fire and thinking: in three days now, and then for two years. But that's okay, it's not twenty-five years. And there's no war. Two years, that's nothing.

The groats swelled and turned white. The girl shook the stewed meat out of the can into the pot and mixed the rose-coloured lumps in with the kasha. She took the pot and the kettle off the hook and poured tea leaves into the kettle. She wiped off her flush moist face and looked at him: I'm doing this pretty well, aren't I?

They ate in the hut, in front of the little window. They ate their smoky-tasting kasha and soft black bread in silence, looking out of the little window. Then they drank the tea. The girl was wondering if it was really true that the city existed somewhere, if it was really true that they'd only left it that morning.

A sharp, crisp, angry shriek echoed from outside; the girl choked, started coughing, and shot a frightened glance at the hut's master.

'It's a peregrine. It lives in the wood. A rare bird.'

The girl nodded. But fright remained in her eyes. After a few moments she said, 'But still, the gun . . . with a gun . . . how on earth did it happen?'

The single-barrelled sixteen-gauge was lying under a thick layer of silt at the bottom of one of the seven Coffee Ponds. But he answered anyway: 'I lost it.'

'Are you lying?'

'No.'

'You're lying,' she said. 'It's so obvious. You're better off never lying. Anyone could tell straight away.'

'Why are you so stuck on that gun?'

'No reason. Just that it would be better to have it.'

'Not better. That I know . . . I threw it in the water.'

'Really?'

'What are you looking at me like that for? Who cares? It was my gun, I bought it, and shells too, from a dealer, and then I decided to throw it in the water.'

'Why?'

'I was tired of it. Even a branch shoots out once a year. A gun much more often. Even if you don't want to shoot anyone.'

They fell silent. The girl sighed.

'Does that worry you?' he asked sarcastically.

'Aha,' she replied. 'In three days you'll be in the army and they won't give you just a gun there, but grenades and a machine-gun.'

'Oh, so that's what it's about . . .'

'I'm perceptive. Aren't I?'

'You certainly are. They will, but so what . . . Three times on a firing range and that's it. Someone I know came back from the army and said that in two years he'd been on a firing range three times, and that was it. Shooting at cardboard men.'

'But they could send you . . .' The girl hesitated.

'Where?'

'Wherever they want, that's where. They could send you to that war. Couldn't they. Vitya?'

He shrugged his shoulders. He poured tea into his cup and sipped it. He had forgotten about the war. Somehow forgotten completely. The newspapers talked about it hazily, sketchily. It was unclear whether Russians were fighting there or planting trees or building kindergartens.

The old bird cried out again, and immediately afterwards a distant, abbreviated sound echoed. A moment later it echoed again.

'A storm?' he asked himself, unsure, and rose from the table to go to the street. The girl smiled, perplexed and happy, and went out too.

The sky over the Village and the wood was spotless. A strong wind struck the birch leaves every now and then. The air felt fresh.

The sun was already low in the west. It was shedding a slanting light on the golden fields, the dappled birch trunks, the rotted, collapsing roofs, the black scraps of fence, the white gardens.

'There,' he said, pointing at the sky over the wood.

'Is that the peregrine?'

A bird with brown plumage and a multicoloured breast was circling overhead.

'Can you smell it,' she asked hoarsely, then cleared her throat, 'the smell of the gardens?'

'Because it's going to rain,' he answered, not looking at her. 'We have to get going. The roads will be soaked.'

In India . . . the tropical rains . . . for weeks, she thought. She was looking helplessly at the sky over the wood, but the sky was spotless.

'Was it okay? Did you like it?' he asked.

She nodded in silence.

'And it wasn't too terrible without the gun?' he asked, smiling.

She shook her head.

'Would you like us to come back in two years?'

'Yes.'

'For a long time?'

She forced herself to smile. 'Yes.'

'Let's get going,' he said, and went back into the hut. He gathered the spoons and cups, picked up the pot and kettle, and walked to the stream.

She remained exactly where she was and watched him walk towards the birches, walking among the birches . . . The trunks and leaves would screen him, he would appear again and then vanish . . . She should have washed the dishes herself, she was thinking, but she didn't move or call out to him. He went further away until he became a mere outline, ghostly. The sun was shining on the birches. The birch trunks were dotted with sharp black stains, burrs, specks. The ancient bird of prey was circling over the treetops.

The edges of storm clouds were gathering over the wood.

He raced back from the wood, rushed into the hut, dropped off the clean dishes, came out, and picked his bicycle up by the handlebars.

'Let's go!'

She followed him obediently. She wanted to say: the rain will start soon, let's stay and wait it out, forget about parents, who cares about them . . . I don't want to think about parents. She walked behind him in silence.

They emerged onto the country road, got on their bikes, and rode off.

The rain sprinkled a little and then stopped. It's too bad, she thought, that Russia doesn't have those tropical rains that last for days, weeks, months.

When they had climbed the hill she look around.

The storm clouds had blown to the south. Above the Village and the wood the sky was blue. The gardens in the Village were white. There, no doubt, the soft grey forest birds were once more trilling and chirruping, trilling and chirruping, flitting from branch to branch and littering the ground with petals.

A Feast on the Bank of a Violet River

All night long, pens were scratching at staff headquarters, and all night long the soldiers who had completed their tours were milling around. All discharges had been postponed for the last three months, and for the whole of that time the soldiers felt as though they had been living alien lives. They went out on raids and sometimes they died. Yesterday they had returned from the usual raid and didn't immediately believe the orders to present themselves, with their service papers, at headquarters. The night was sultry and moonless, the stars hung like lanterns in the sky, the cicadas had gone crazy, dust wafted off the steppes, a smell of disinfectant rose from the long, wagon-like latrines, and from time to time the forward guard regiment fired off short bursts of tracer to ward off sleep – this last night was routine, but to those smoking and waiting their turn on the headquarters steps it seemed insane.

Morning came, and everyone being transferred to the reserves fell in on the parade ground.

They were waiting for the regimental commander. The headquarters doors opened and out onto the steps came some sort of officer or messenger, but the commander himself was not to be seen.

But then, accompanied by an escort of majors and lieutenant-colonels, all of them stocky, sunburned, and sullen, the commander came down the steps. The parade ground fell silent. The commander walked slowly, limping on his left leg and leaning on a freshly carved cane. On his last operation he had jumped down clumsily from an armoured transport and wrenched a tendon, but almost no one knew about his unfortunate mishap. The commander shuffled along, wincing slightly. Thinking that he had been shot, everyone looked at his wounded leg and his cane with respect.

The commander came to a halt in the middle of the square and glanced around at the soldiers.

This severe fellow will now say a few uncharacteristically warm words, everyone thought, and the throats of the more sentimental began to tighten.

After stopping and looking around, the commander pointed his cane in the direction of a lanky red-headed soldier standing in front of him.

'Come here,' the commander said.

The soldier, who was wearing a makeshift uniform that had been crimped and altered to suit his tastes, left the ranks, clicked his heels, raised his hand to the small, trimmed-back visor of his officer's cap, and stated his name and unit. The commander looked him up and down in silence. The soldier shifted from foot to foot and stared guiltily at the white wooden cane.

'What are you, a ballerina?' said the commander, grimacing in disgust.

The commander did not manage to address a farewell speech to his soldiers: while he was yelling at the officers for not keeping an eye on what the soldiers were doing to their dress uniforms, while he was screaming at one soldier, 'What are you, a ballerina?' while he was screaming at all the soldiers, 'Are you ballerinas or soldiers, you motherfuckers?' the report came in from Kabul that the helicopters had taken off, and an adjutant hurried out onto the square to inform him of the fact. The commander fell silent, waved his hand, and ordered the vehicles to be brought up.

The Mi-6, a heavy, cumbersome helicopter, couldn't land at the camp – it needed solid ground to take off from, and although work on a landing strip had begun, it hadn't been followed through and finished. And so covered trucks under the protection of two armoured transports had to drive the demobilized soldiers to the provincial centre, where there was a military airfield.

It was no more than ten miles from the camp to the city and the road ran through flat empty steppe, so there was no danger of attack. The only thing was that the commander had forgotten to have the way cleared by a sweeper – a heavily armoured vehicle, a little like a tank, that clears a road of mines. His leg was aching and he had too much else to do: in two days the regiment was to set out for Kandahar.

The machines tore down the dusty road, carefully avoiding craters old and new.

Along the road were green fields of potato and grain and long rows of dusty, pyramidal poplars. The column reached the city and everyone looked at it for the last time: at the earthen houses, towers, *duvals*, at the yellowish irrigation ditches, the muddy sewers and implausible gardens with their streams, flowerbeds, lawns, and arbours, at the domed mosques and the earthen, ornamental, flower-covered fingers of the minarets, at the *dukan* stalls piled up with all kinds of multicoloured wares, at the small horses decorated with paper ribbons and harnessed to light carriages, at the ragged, bearded, barefoot beggars resting in the shade of plane-trees, at the women in chadors, at the young boys hawking cigarettes and condoms, at donkeys laden with bundles of kindling . . .

On the airfield the staff and regimental officers who had accompanied the demobilized soldiers drew the men up into ranks and began what the soldiers called the 'frisk'. The officers ordered everyone to empty their bags, 'diplomats', and pockets and lay everything out on the ground. They moved through the ranks briskly, forcing one man to squeeze out his tube of toothpaste, palpating another man's sling or his cap. They didn't find any hash on anyone. They did, however, find and confiscate a Koran, a string of rosary beads, a pack of pornographic playing cards, and a Pakistani newspaper containing photos of hunted-looking prisoners surrounded by grinning, moustachioed men in turbans. From Ninidze they took five pairs of German sunglasses, considering that a bit too many. Ninidze grew heated and tried to argue that he wasn't planning on being a speculator, he was just bringing them back for friends. The noise attracted a lieutenant from the special section, a man with a pale sweaty face and thick, wrinkled eyelids rimmed in red.

'What is your name?' he asked Ninidze. He was the only officer in the whole regiment who addressed the soldiers formally. He was gazing placidly at Ninidze, who lost all inclination to argue that he wanted something nice to give to his friends. But Ninidze explained what they were for anyway.

The lieutenant took out his handkerchief, wiped his pale face, and asked, 'Where did you get that Japanese thing?'

'Which one?'

'That one, that radio.'

'I bought it,' answered Ninidze, blanching.

'The receipt.'

Ninidze ventured with a smile, 'What receipt? I bought it from a *dukan*, they don't give you receipts.'

The lieutenant picked up the radio and examined it. To Ninidze it seemed that he was about to sniff the radio with his bony nose.

'You bought it,' the officer muttered. 'You bought it. But it could be . . . couldn't it?'

'What?'

'Anything.'

'No,' Ninidze objected, 'this thing, I bought it.'

The lieutenant smiled a sickly smile.

'Yes? Shall we find out?'

'How?'

'Very simple. For that we must return to camp.'

'You're joking,' said Ninidze.

'No, I'm not joking at all.'

'Comrade first-lieutenant,' said Romanov, a brown-eyed high-cheekboned, thickset sergeant.

The lieutenant looked at him.

'Comrade first-lieutenant, we've been together, us five, from the beginning to the end,' said Romanov, nodding his head towards Ninidze and the men around him.

'I understand,' the officer retorted. 'You're right – the five of you should return to camp. It will turn up, what needs to be found out. Where are you from? The reconnaissance company? Well, boys . . .'

'That's not necessary, comrade lieutenant,' said Romanov.

'Not necessary?' The officer slid a glance over the men around Romanov, lingered on the lustreless eyes of the small, runty Reyutov, looked at Romanov again and asked him: 'Why is he stoned?'

'Who?' Romanov answered in a surprised voice.

'That one there.' The officer pointed towards Reyutov with his eyes. 'Are you stoned?' he asked Reyutov.

'No,' Reyutov replied.

The lieutenant fell silent for half a minute. While he was silent the demobs from the reconnaissance company imagined having to drive back to camp again and see its trenches, its depots, its long latrines, the rows of weatherproofed tents; hear how the captain would let out a whistle when he saw them and the Zampolit would say: I warned you, I really warned you, that sooner or later every secret would come out.

'Well then,' sighed the lieutenant. He fell silent again and glanced over the soldiers' heads. And everyone heard the rumbling clatter, turned their heads, and saw the black objects in the sky above the grey-blue mountains.

'Yes. It is in fact a lot of sunglasses,' Ninidze muttered.

The lieutenant looked at him happily.

'There we go,' he said.

'Yes. Exactly,' Ninidze added.

'And you?' The officer turned to face Reyutov. 'What do you have to say?'

'I don't smoke hash.'

The clatter was growing louder; the objects had passed the mountains, were already moving across the potato and grain fields on the outskirts of the city, and were becoming longer and thicker.

All the demobs who had already been dismissed were talking loudly among themselves, beating dust out of their jackets and service caps, and, keeping their distance, watching the rangers and the regiment's lieutenant.

An infantry major on leave who was accompanying the group as far as Tashkent walked up to him and called out, 'Comrade lieutenant.'

'We're not really sure what to do: return to camp or fly to the Union,' the lieutenant responded.

The major raised his eyebrows.

'Something serious?' he asked, looking up. The helicopters were about to land.

'There's always something serious. Everyone has something serious.'

The major looked intently at the lieutenant, then glanced away.

The helicopters landed and started to trundle heavily and clumsily down the airfield. The wind picked up and the soldiers clutched at their caps.

'What now?' the major shouted, holding on to his cap and turning away from the wind.

'All right,' the lieutenant answered with a condescending smile. 'But that one there, the stoned one, he could stand a lesson.' He menaced Reyutov with a finger. 'All right, fine,' he said, and walked off towards the officers standing around a small white stone house on the edge of the airfield.

Romanov couldn't restrain himself and swore. The major didn't catch what he said, although from Romanov's lips he gathered what it was and shook his head. But what he had said was about right and the infantry major had to smile.

In Kabul the helicopters managed to land just before the whole valley was engulfed in a *samoum*. The soldiers climbed out of the helicopters and immediately looked at the giant winged machine that they'd spotted from the air, painted white and blue, with 'Tu-134' written on its side. Then they turned their heads to the east and their eyes popped: moving noiselessly down the valley from the east, shutting off the sky and the mountains and their colourless, shimmering glaciers, carpeting the gardens and hillsides covered in earthen dwellings, was something shaggy and brown; it was still windless on the airfield and the sun was shining in the deep blue sky, but right nearby everything was impenetrable and foreboding, which was why the approaching *samoum* seemed to be something supernatural and filled with doom, like the sounding of the seven trumpets.

When all the soldiers were out of the helicopters the major led them across the airfield to the transit camp. The camp, surrounded by barbed wire, was not far from the airfield, at the foot of mountains that were hot and scorched below and cold, blue-grey, swathed in snow and glaciers above.

'Faster!' the major shouted, and everyone, casting glances at the city, hurried behind him.

The city was already half-engulfed in the *samoum*; the soldiers could already make out the dustclouds, and they saw the whirlwinds driving pieces of paper, leaves, and all sorts of grey scraps and tatters of rag. The major was hurrying, everyone was hurrying, treading sharply across the concrete. They were hurrying along, clutching their caps in their hands. They were hurrying along behind their rapidly striding major, but the yellow shadow of the *samoum* already lay over them. Halfway there the brown blizzard caught them.

They lost their way and only after an hour – lashed by sand and stones, caked with dust, angry, gasping for breath – did they find themselves at the transit station. The camp commander assigned them tents. The tents were filled with dust too, but the sandy wind no longer cut into them and burned their faces, stones no longer struck them in the head, and, most important, they were finally able to smoke.

The *samoum* died down late at night. In the camp everyone but the guards was asleep. The camp was full of soldiers being transferred to the reserves and of new recruits, all of them asleep, all dreaming different dreams, and in their dreams all hoping for different things: the demobs believing that tomorrow they would fly out of here for ever, the recruits thinking of benevolent commanders, benevolent old-timers, and places where there wouldn't be much shooting.

In the middle of the night the alarm on Ninidze's wristwatch beeped. Ninidze awoke, got up, left the tent, looked around. It was quiet, dark, and above him the stars glimmered blue, green, and red. A few rare lights were burning in the capital. Above the city rose the dark mountaintops. Ninidze went back in, drew his transistor radio from his 'diplomat', threw his jacket over his bare body, shoved the radio under the jacket, went out of the tent, and, glancing around, headed towards the furthest end of the camp.

He was walking towards the furthest end of the camp, carrying the radio in his breast, where it was sticking to his sweaty chest, and entreating his Old Man to make sure he didn't run into the duty officer.

He met no one and reached his goal, a long wood-planked building. He walked through the narrow door and froze – he had seen a lighted cigarette in the darkness. He wanted to leap away right then, but he recollected himself, went to the rear wall, found a hole, dropped his pants, and sat down. His neighbour was silent, smoking and occasionally spitting. Ninidze sat and waited. Finally his neighbour left, and after waiting for a bit Ninidze drew out his sweat-soaked trophy and dropped it into the hole. The radio fell with a loud plop.

Ninidze returned to his tent, undressed, and lay down on his bare iron frame – for fear of fleas they had stripped all the mattresses from the bunks and stacked them in a corner. He listened tensely for a few minutes, but nothing could be heard except the heavy breathing and snores of his neighbours, so he let himself relax, sighed deeply, entreated his Old Man to make sure they would fly out in the morning, and fell asleep.

Morning came, sunny.

After breakfast a large party of demobs was taken to the airfield. Those left behind could see, through the barbed wire, when an hour later the party was seated in the aircraft, could see the aircraft go down the runway, pick up speed, break away from the grey concrete and rise up into the air, make a half-turn over the city, and fly away to the north.

Those left behind were sitting in the smoking areas, going through one cigarette after another, and sullenly watching the recruits, who seemed like some sort of mock soldiers to them, flown in here not to fight but to act in a play about war: their faces were so fresh and clear, and they were so unconvincing in their attempts to hide their terror, laughing and joking forcedly, frowning and swearing copiously. But however coarsely and shamelessly they swore, however much they frowned and postured, it was obvious that the recruits were terrified and had no idea as to how they would endure for two years what these sunburned, moustachioed men in their caps and insignia-covered and bemedalled jackets had endured.

There were no more large aircraft to be seen on the airfield, and the demobs were saying to each other, 'Right, let's catch some sun.'

But at midday a transport plane landed and someone remembered that a friend who had flown out a year before had written that his group had flown home in a cargo plane, and everyone came alive and started to argue if it was true or not.

Half an hour went by. The infantry major appeared. He gathered his group and led it to the camp gates. Here some captain or other, wearing glasses, read the roll call and everyone in the group cried out: 'Present! Present! Present!'

Another half-hour went by. The soldiers stood obediently in front of the gate under the full sunlight. Sweat streamed down their faces. The soldiers stood and humbly watched their major, who was smoking off to one side. But then the captain in the eyeglasses appeared again and everyone fixed their eyes on him. The captain nodded to the major, walked to the head of the line, ordered the guards to open the gate, and the guards opened the gate, the officer motioned with his hand, and the soldiers walked out.

The officers in the customs shed, all of them very young, turned out to be pleasant and lenient. They examined things less quickly and efficiently than the regimental searchers had, squeezing out only one of the many tubes of toothpaste and only cutting open a couple of bars of soap. In one of the bars was an Afghani banknote. The officers laughed: What do you need this for in the Union? As a memento, the soldier answered. The officers gave back the piece of paper. They didn't find hash on anyone. In truth they didn't go out of their way to look for it. They paid no attention at all to sunglasses, jeans, Pakistani cigarettes, and so on, even though it had been said at the transit station that they were beasts in customs at Kabul, nothing like the searchers at one's own regiment – you could kiss goodbye to anything that didn't come from a Soviet store.

Ninidze was gloomy when they went out of the customs shed and headed towards the cargo plane.

'What's up with you, Murman?' asked Romanov.

Ninidze remained silent.

'Murman,' Romanov called out again. 'Hey, Murman, come on, you'll drink some booze today.'

Ninidze smiled sadly.

'No, probably not today,' corrected Shingarev.

'But he'll taste some nice Tashkent wine,' said Romanov, 'today.'

'Sasha and I only drink vodka,' said the hefty and broad-shouldered Spivakov in his deep voice. 'Right, Sasha?'

The small Reyutov smiled but said nothing.

'We'll drink everything,' said Romanov. 'But the wine has to be red. It's the wine of victory. Isn't that so, Shingarev-Holmes?'

'Yes.' Shingarev, the lapsed student, nodded his head. The nickname had been bestowed on him by courtesy of the captain: when he had been wounded in the buttocks by bullet fragments at Kandahar and began to moan, the captain comforted him by saying that Sherlock had been wounded at Kandahar too.

'We'll drink everything, wine and vodka,' Romanov repeated.

'And beer,' someone said.

'And women too!' someone else in the group exclaimed.

'Hey, is nookie expensive in Tashkent?'

'Forty, if the client doesn't have a face like a brick wall.'

'And if he does?'

'Fifty.'

'Bloody opportunists! Back in Tokmak they'd give themselves for a bar of chocolate!'

They came to a halt, laughing, in front of the cargo plane. The major on leave walked towards the pilots standing in the shade of the wings. After talking to them for a few moments he came back and said that the plane hadn't been unloaded yet and that they would, once more, have to do their bit for the army.

'So we have to wait for a truck now?' they asked him cheerlessly.

'No, we'll stack it all here on the ground.'

'We're sick of loading and unloading. This is brutal. We're free men, for Christ's sake,' someone said.

'You shut up, free man,' the others broke in. 'We'll unload it, comrade major, no problem.'

'Why don't you all just unload it,' the 'free man' was heard to say.

The major broke into a stream of obscenities and asked if any of them wanted to go home at all; stripping to the waist, everyone went off to unload the plane.

They heaved out and set down to the side of the aircraft cases, sacks, boxes, and bluish, foul-smelling sheep carcasses. They scurried up and down the gangway, heaving, dragging out cases, boxes, sacks, and carcasses, and the sun was scorching their bare heads and their backs were shining with sweat.

After they unloaded the aircraft they wiped themselves down with their hankerchiefs and put their shirts and jackets back on.

Then they climbed into the hot aircraft and scattered to sit along the fuselage; there weren't enough seats, and the slower ones ended up having to settle on their bags and 'diplomats' or on newspapers. Reyutov managed to find a place next to a porthole, but just then a round-faced artilleryman came up to him and simply said, 'Let me sit there.'

Reyutov stared at him with his dull eyes.

'Just try sitting there,' said Spivakov.

The artilleryman glanced at Spivakov and silently moved away.

'Pansy gunner,' Spivakov muttered with a smirk.

A little while later the pilots in their clean and beautiful pale blue suits entered the cabin, and after a few minutes the gangway in the tail section rose smoothly and the dim ceiling lights overhead lit up.

The aircraft lurched and started to roll gently down the runway.

Breathing was difficult. Their faces shone in the stifling semi-darkness and looked almost black. The place stank of sweat and sheep-meat.

The aircraft began to shudder and everyone tensed up as though it was they who had to gather their strength, break into a sprint, and leap into the air. The aircraft hurtled off, rose, filling up with gravity, and suddenly started gliding smoothly, and everyone knew that it had taken off, that they were flying away for ever.

Tashkent, the city of women, was illuminated by the rays of the evening sun. Its east-facing windows were shining; in its shady and – especially at this hour – verdant gardens innumerable fountains were gurgling coolly. Tashkent was noisy, vast, tall; well-dressed people with well-fed faces, untroubled, unclouded, were walking along its streets. It was a city of feminine eyes, hair, lips. Women were everywhere the demobs looked: in shop windows, on buses, in cars, in house windows, doorways, stalls – they saw women everywhere, women young, middle-aged, old, girls, women full-figured, ugly, narrow-hipped, Rubenesque, almond-eyed, wide-eyed, dark-haired, red-haired, women with beauty spots on their cheeks, bare-shouldered, in skirts, in transparent gowns. In short it was an amazing city and in its streets the demobs felt, more than anything, just like the recruits at the transit camp in Kabul.

They were going crazy and didn't know where to go or what to do next. They had been to the airport and the railway station and learned that tickets to where they had to go were all sold out for nearly the whole of the coming week, and now they plodded down the streets, stopping at yellow barrels to gulp down kvass, arguing and debating what to do. Spivakov suggested saying to hell with it all, buying vodka, and finding some secluded corner where they could have a good party. Shingarev retorted: What if a patrol caught them? The idea of sitting in a Tashkent cooler didn't please anyone, and everyone except Spivakov hesitated: to drink or not to drink.

They were walking through the streets, arguing and debating, falling silent whenever they came across a girl or woman and staring her up and down from head to toe.

Ninidze proposed buying their tickets and living in a hotel for a week. They rejected this fantastic notion out of hand – what hotel? Spivakov was saying over and over to everyone that the best thing to do would be to buy some vodka, find some secluded place, get drunk, and only in the morning try to work out what was what. Shingarev suggested bribing a conductor and riding in betweeen the carriages, if need be, to Orenburg: from there it had to be easier to fly out or catch a train to Tblisi, Moscow, Kuibishev, Rostov-on-Don, and Minsk, and they could have their party on the train without fear of any patrol. This satisfied everyone. Ninidze instantly painted a picture of the woman conductor they'd be negotiating with: youngish plump, with pink ears and cheeks and no prejudice at all.

They returned to the station.

On the way to the station they went into a shop and bought canned fish, fishcakes, bread, cucumbers, wine, and vodka. '*Bon appetit*, boys,' said the woman behind the counter, a red-head with thick lips.

'Cor, what shameless eyes,' Ninidze groaned when they had gone out.

*

They loitered around on the platforms until dark, talking to conductors and promising them at first fifty roubles, then seventy-five, a hundred – but they were turned down.

It fell completely dark, and Spivakov was saying that he'd done enough begging when the arrival of another train was announced and they decided to try their luck once more.

The train arrived, its brakes squealed and it came to a halt, and a noisy throng of people rushed to the carriages, but the demobs hurried towards the last one – for some reason it seemed to them that it was more fitting for outlaws to ride in the last carriage. They hurried to the last one and Ninidze entreated his Old Man, 'Please, make it that . . .'

People were stretching tickets out to a greying, corpulent conductor. In the side of his mouth the conductor was holding a cheap cigarette. He would puff on the cigarette, take a ticket, palm it, stick his palm in the light coming in through the door, hand the ticket back, and nod his head: Pass.

The crowd around him thinned out, and Shingarev said to the conductor confidentially, 'We have this idea . . .'

The conductor took all the soldiers in with a quick glance and growled,

'Well?'

'This is the idea.'

'What?'

'The idea is, we'll pay you – ' Shingarev began.

'Oh no, oh no,' the conductor interrupted him.

' – a hundred roubles – '

'No.' The conductor looked at his watch. 'That's it, the matter's closed.'

He turned around and strode onto the connecting walkway between the carriages.

'Were you ever in the army, grandpa? You must have been in the forces sometime. Listen, this thing here . . .'

From the walkway the conductor glanced over their heads to the platform, in case some straggler was rushing to make it aboard, and without answering Shingarev he began to close the heavy door. The door was nearly shut when at the last moment Romanov stuck his boot in the crack.

'Hey!' The conductor let out an astonished yell and flung the door open.

'Will you answer me like a human being?' Romanov said.

With a kick the conductor knocked Romanov's foot off the step and slammed the door. Romanov started hitting the thick dusty glass with his fists. The conductor stood on the other side of the door and looked at them. He took out his pack of cigarettes, drew one out, blew into the cardboard mouthpiece, lit up, and again stared at the soldiers. The train pulled out shortly afterwards and Romanov spat on the dirty window.

When the train had moved some way off the conductor opened the door and screamed: 'Shitbags!'

After roaming for a while in the vicinity of the station they came across a park. There was a river there, narrow and straight. The river gave off a faint reek but they decided it was nothing and settled themselves down by the water. From time to time people passed through the park, but they were screened from their eyes by the bushes running along the banks. Along the opposite bank extended the blind walls of some squat brick edifice over which lamp posts towered, casting a violet light on the dark roof, the river, and the soldiers. They were glad to discover how light and yet secluded it was here. They were even happier when they had spread newspapers on the grass and on them laid out the bread, the canned food, the cucumbers – and when they looked at the colonnade of bottles sparkling so brightly.

'Not a bad little restaurant,' Spivakov said.

Everyone was quick to agree that the little restaurant was just fine.

'Then let's get at it,' Spivakov said. He had set out little paper cups and was reaching for a bottle of vodka when Shingarev stopped him.

'The port first.'

'I don't want to mix, I just want vodka,' Spivakov answered.

'No, we have to drink the port first.'

'No one tells me I have to do anything any more.'

'It was agreed. We agreed to drink red wine, it's the wine of victory,' Shingarev insisted.

Romanov and Ninidze backed Shingarev up, and Spivakov conceded. Shingarev poured the port out into cups. They raised their cups, brimming over with dark wine, carefully toasted with them, and drained them. On the next round Shingarev choked and started coughing. He put his empty cup down and raised his hands to his chest.

'I've spilled it on myself, shit,' he managed to force out, and again started coughing.

'It's nothing, *bidzho*,' replied Ninidze, leaning towards him and examining his shirt.

'Feels pretty sticky,' Shingarev retorted.

Romanov lit a cigarette and raised the burning match to Shingarev's chest, and everyone saw the big dark stain on his shirt.

'Wash it out,' Ninidze advised.

'Then he'll have to wash the whole shirt,' Romanov said.

'It'll get wrinkled and where can I iron it? Christ . . .'

'Nonsense, just brush it down,' said Spivakov.

Romanov threw out an idea. 'Maybe if you put your tie on.'

Shingarev drew his tie from the pocket of his jacket, which was lying off to the side on his 'diplomat', and put it on.

'Well, how's that?'

'Give us some light.'

Romanov lit a match. 'You can barely see it. If you keep your jacket on, no one will even notice it, probably.'

'Just forget about the damn clothes. I say to hell with them. Me and Sasha say to hell with them, right Sasha?' Spivakov asked.

Sasha Reyutov's narrow violet face wrinkled – as always, he smiled without a sound. Spivakov poured some vodka for himself and Reyutov and asked if he should pour some for the others. Ninidze and Romanov nodded but Shingarev declined. They drank the vodka and, puffing loudly, set into the food. Shingarev drank port.

All the same to me, Spivakov continued his train of thought. Me and Sasha will ride in our underpants as long as it's homeward, eh Sasha?

It was the middle of the night. People had stopped coming through the park. The violet river lay still between its banks. The sounds of the railway could be heard easily: the indifferent voice on the loudspeaker, whistles, the crack of coupling carriages, wheels clicking, diesels rumbling.

Ninidze, who had suddenly forgotten how to speak proper Russian, was cursing the lieutenant from the special section, cursing the staff officer who had confiscated the sunglasses, cursing all the authorities for not allowing them a normal return home; he flew into a rage and started screaming in Georgian. But no one was listening. Spivakov was still regretting that he had been too scared to bring a couple of slabs of hash in his shoulder-pouch or his boot-soles – he claimed that vodka didn't do anything for him, he said he was so used to hash that vodka seemed like water; he too was cursing the lieutanant who had slandered Sasha Reyutov – Sasha, who never in his life had tasted the sweet herb, hash. Romanov was chain-smoking, showering himself with ash, and looking warmly at his comrades. From time to time he would tilt his head back and stare at the poplar trees illuminated by the blue-violet light of the lamp posts: he stared for ages, smiling, at the poplars. The only one still sober was Shingarev, who was straining his ears and peering around.

It was the middle of the night. The poplars and the violet, motionless river had fallen silent. From somewhere beyond the sleeping houses came the sounds of the railway.

'Murman,' said Romanov, lighting another cigarette. 'Hey, come on, stop cursing. Such a day . . . a night. And you, Shingarev-Holmes, I swear I don't even want to look at you. Drink some vodka and get rid of that paint.'

'Someone has to stay sober,' Shingarev replied.

'Here? What, here, on a night like this?' Romanov leaned his head back and fell silent, staring at the sky.

'Get drunk, Shingarev-Holmes,' said Spivakov. 'It's not doing anything for me. I'm sober as a judge.'

Romanov roused himself. 'Should we sing? Something soulful. "We're not diplomats by afoca . . ." Fo . . . How does it go? You're not diplomats by afoca . . . Fo, fo! Ha-ha! Afocation! Ha-ha!'

'No, that won't do for music,' Spivakov said. 'But hey, Murman, get out your made-in-Japan.'

Murman-Ninidze said gloomily, 'The radio ain't, someone stole it.'

'What? How, who?'

'At the transit station, zip, zap, gone!'

'Why didn't you say something?' Romanov yelled.

'What, what? What could've I said?'

'What, what do you mean, what? We would have beaten the daylights out of them all! All those dogs! What do you mean, what? All of them . . . those scum, the bast . . . All my life, that conductor . . . his face, in a hundred years . . . I'll rip the damn thing off!' Romanov yelled.

'The foolishness begins,' said Spivakov, frowning.

'Don't shout,' Shingarev said to Romanov. 'And why all this about the conductor?'

'What? Why are you always afraid of everything? Let them come over to us. Just let them.' Romanov hit his palm with his fist. 'A patrol, the cops. They want to start something with recce? Just let them!' Romanov hit his palm with his fist harder and faster.

'Strange,' muttered Spivakov. 'How could it have happened? Murman, you were asleep on your "diplomat" and you didn't go anywhere at night, did you? Then how did they pull it off?'

'Some sort of devilry,' Ninidze answered, lifting his hands.

He felt someone looking at him, glanced to the side, and saw a narrow face lit up in the violet light: dark wrinkles, long bony nose, thin dark lips, the dark patch of its eyes. 'If Reyutov knows something, make it so he stays quiet,' Ninidze entreated his Old Man. It had become a habit – to entreat someone, someone he imagined as grey-haired, intelligent, powerful, generous, some-one he called Old Man – since his first raid: he had been in an extremely tight situation and somehow he unexpectedly said, 'Old Man, make it so . . .' and he had made it out of that scrape without a single scratch.

Reyutov said nothing. He was even staring off to the side somewhere. How could Reyutov know anything? Ninidze relaxed.

'It went the way it came,' Shingarev said all of a sudden.

'What d'you mean?'

'It went the way it came,' Shingarev repeated coldly.

'How'd it come?'

'You know how.'

'What you trying to say?'

'He needs a drink, quick.' Romanov pointed his finger at Shingarev.

'I understand,' Spivakov said. 'I can see right through these chickens.'

'Lads!' Romanov waved his hands. 'Don't! Let's drink instead.'

'Nah, talk,' demanded Ninidze.

'Drop it, drop it,' Shingarev muttered.

'No, talk, tell us everything, Shingarev!'

'I know what it is,' said Spivakov. 'He's been wanting to say it for a long time, I've seen it. He's been a chicken from the very start. This is what he's been wanting to say, he's been wanting to say that we're bringing trophies home and he isn't. That's it, isn't it? I don't care. Those things we got in the war, I couldn't care less about them, understand?'

'There we go!' Ninidze exclaimed. 'That's it! That's what he's gettin' at. That what you gettin' at? You're too good, eh?'

Shingarev's mouth was already open to acknowledge, yes, yes, that's what I've been wanting to say, but he unexpectedly glanced at Reyutov, he was struck by some thought about Reyutov, and he announced, softly, 'I didn't want to say anything like that.'

'Men. Lads.' Romanov picked up a bottle. 'Such a day . . . a night.' He became pensive.

'You asleep? Pour it,' Spivakov growled, sticking out his cup.

'Wait . . . it was . . . I was thinking . . . The thing I wanted to say . . .'

'Pour, will you?'

'No, but . . .' Romanov shook his head. 'No, I forget.' He

poured vodka into the cups, more or less. 'Come on, let's just drink, that's it, no more about all this . . . To hell with it! Liberty, that's the thing. And that's all . . . these tricks and turns . . . these quarrels, to hell with them. But liberty – yes! But! That wasn't what I was thinking, it's gone, vanished.'

Romanov was sitting, his cup in his hands, frowning, his eyes rooted to the centre of the 'table', his lips moving; the vodka overflowed the edge of his cup and ran down his hand.

'Drink it, don't spill it.'

Romanov glanced absently at Spivakov, drank down his vodka without a wince, and burst out: 'Hey! I remember! I have this feeling – ' he looked around ' – this feeling . . . that someone's missing.'

'Of course someone's missing,' Spivakov mumbled.

'No, no, it's not that, not them.'

'Okay, lie down, go to sleep.'

'No, you have to understand.'

'Look, just lie down, lie down, sleep, the ground's warm.'

'You don't understand. I'm saying that someone isn't with us – he was, but now he isn't.' Romanov looked at those sitting around the 'table'.

'Lie down,' said Spivakov. 'We're all here.'

Romanov looked around at his comrades, finally noticed Reyutov, and froze. He was looking at Reyutov with wide-open eyes, saying nothing. He remained silent for a long time. Everyone was quiet, watching him and Reyutov.

'Ah!' Romanov shouted. 'Ah, Reyutov! Sashka! Ha-ha! Well! Ha-ha-ha!'

'Just like I said – foolishness,' growled Spivakov.

Romanov stopped laughing. 'Everyone,' he said, 'Everyone gathered, and the feast . . . it . . . continues. They're feasting . . . these . . . ex-recces.' Romanov took a deep breath and started to sing: 'We were marching so far a-away, Where almost no one's ever gone! We were waiting in ambush for years . . .' He fell silent. His eyes found Reyutov and fixed on him.

Reyutov's narrow violet face covered with furrows – he was smiling.

'It's me,' he said to Romanov. 'Don't worry.'

'Sasha,' Romanov uttered in a raw voice. 'Sasha . . . an amazing thing . . . you understand.' He fell silent. 'I just remembered . . . how we were flown in to the regiment.'

'And what?' asked Spivakov.

'What?' Romanov pulled himself together. 'Nothing! Just amazing. Amazing . . . it was . . . it. And everyone . . . We were waiting in ambush for years, Despite the snow and the rain!'

Yes, that's exactly what I was thinking about too, Shingarev said to himself. I was thinking, I was thinking. I'm drunk anyway. Have to concentrate and remember how we were flown in to the regiment. He concentrated and remembered how they had been flown in to the regiment after three months of training in a camp in the mountains of Turkmenistan; out of the crowd of recruits the commander of the reconnaissance company had chosen the enormous Spivakov first, and Spivakov had said that the five of them were sticking together, and he asked the commander to take the others. The commander gladly agreed to take the wiry, lithe Ninidze, the strong, broad-shouldered Romanov, and him, Shingarev, but Reyutov he flatly refused. Well, Spivakov said to Reyutov, do something Rostov-on-Donnish, but he started to say no, Spivakov pressed him, and finally the captain became interested in whatever it was this puny boy could 'do'. Seeing curiosity on the captain's face, everyone turned on Reyutov, and Reyutov, blushing, sang one Kazakhstani *chastushka*. The captain's heavy face crumpled into a smile, he asked what else Reyutov could do, and Reyutov innocently answered that he could play the accordion and knew a million *chastushkas*; the captain asked him again – a million? – and enlisted Reyutov in the recce company.

'So, still think you too good?' asked Ninidze, moving toward Shingarev.

'Shut it,' said Romanov.

'I'll calm them down right now, I'll brain them right now.' Spivakov tried to stand but couldn't. He looked at his legs, puzzled, and called to them: 'Legs!'

Romanov burst out laughing. Even Ninidze smiled. Spivakov attempted it again, rose, stood for a moment, wobbling, and sat back down heavily.

'My legs.' He threw up his hands and everyone started laughing, and Reyutov's narrow face soundlessly wrinkled.

'And you said vodka did nothin' for yer.'

'Traitors,' Spivakov said to his legs.

'Quiet!' Romanov shouted. 'Quiet! Umm . . .' He hit himself on the forehead. 'Shit, shit! I forget . . . what a toast, and I've lost it.'

'Fine, let's just drink.' Spivakov grabbed the bottle, held it up to his cup, and dropped it. 'Agh! This is really foolishness! And my right hand – the same thing! A traitor.'

'Quiet!' Romanov shouted again. 'The toast, here it is. Let's drink to . . . that is, to, that is, that! That our hands and legs may betray us, but never our friends!'

Spivakov approved. 'What a toast!'

'And now give him your hand,' Romanov demanded of Shingarev, 'your hand to Murman.'

'We weren't fighting,' Shingarev answered.

'Is it so hard to shake hands?'

Shingarev remained silent.

'Agh, idiots.' Romanov turned towards the river. Suddenly he started to take off his shirt. 'Who'll go swimming with me?' he asked in a businesslike voice.

'I won't let you,' Spivakov said.

'We'll see about that. We've yet to see, as they say. The old recce man will go bathing. He will bathe. That's it. I'm sick of you all. Do your head-butting without me, my rams. But I will swim,' said Romanov.

'Where to?' Spivakov asked sarcastically.

'Far away, that's all. Oh, you'll butt away here and you'll be gored by a ram. Or a mosquito. Or a bull. A big bull with a muzzle like this: Mooo!'

Shingarev was the last to fall asleep.

By early morning everyone was sleeping, but Shingarev held out: rubbing his eyes, shaking his head, smoking, pacing to and fro. But even he fell asleep.

They were sleeping around the ravaged 'table'. Ninidze was lying, covered by his jacket, with his head on his 'diplomat'. Romanov, naked to the waist, lay on his back with his arms sprawled out; he was shivering and grinding his teeth. Reyutov was lying nestled against the large, hot, hoarse-breathing Spivakov. Shingarev slept sitting, his head on his knees.

At dawn the poplars, silent all night, started to rustle. Ripples appeared on the river.

A warm rain descended on the city.

The rain tapped against bottles, empty cans of food, matchboxes, against the black crust of an uneaten loaf of bread, 'diplomats', cap-visors; the newspapers disintegrated and the cigarette butts strewn among them turned black and swelled.

Without waking up, Ninidze pulled his jacket over his head. Reyutov pressed himself into Spivakov's side. No one else moved.

Safe Return

The giant general grinned and said that Orshev was going to be in the regiment for ever now; Orshev would try to sneak away but the general always caught him, and Orshev decided to kill the general – he would steal up to him, now in the form of a snake, now in the form of an old man, a child, a woman, a tank, but the general would always recognize him and hide behind an iron door: Orshev was hallucinating under his damp sheets. He was hunting some general, feasting with black, swollen, foul-smelling corpses on a white mountaintop; becoming light as a wood-shaving, terrified of the wind, then suddenly heavy as a granite monument and sinking up to his knees into the earth; sometimes he could see his lungs, transparent sacks tightly packed with worms; he'd run into his house and throw a grenade into a cake lying on a feast-day table, and leap out through the door, then lean his weight against it, and his friends, parents, and children would scream and pound on the door, but he wouldn't let them out and the grenade exploded; or he'd race around a garden, naked, after a nimble old woman, someone else would help him catch her, and both of them, snarling and biting at each other, would fall on her . . .

Orshev was hallucinating in the stuffy, overcrowded ward of a medical unit, and at the same time the last group of soldiers bound for the reserves was flying to Kabul. The men he had been living beside for two years had flown away for ever. They had wanted to return to Russia together. For two years the return home had been their favourite topic: they would imagine out loud, with relish, on night-guard duty or after a battle or around a fire behind the bathhouses – where in the evening they usually cooked up some potatoes, drank tea, and smoked hash – they would spend hours imagining how they would walk down the gangway in Tashkent, jingling their medals, buy cognac, sit down in the train and start drinking, laughing and remembering, and terrified women would huddle in the corners, their mouths open, listening and watching while they – wiry, sunburned, daring – drank, laughed, and remembered the war.

But this is how it turned out:

On the last operation – for three weeks the battalion, along with government troops, had besieged the Urgan gorge – the soldiers went swimming after their umpteenth sortie into the mountains. The river was fast, clear, and cold; the muddy, sweaty soldiers had climbed into the torrent, lain back, and let it pull them under, then they jumped out of the river and sprawled out on the hot white sand; their cooled bodies grown hot again, the soldiers would once more climb into the water. Orshev stayed in the river longer than anyone else – his stupid idea had been to soak up enough cold and liquid to last until night without him feeling either heat or thirst. He found a submerged boulder in the middle of the river, grabbed hold of it, stretched himself out, and let the water rock him up and down and shake him from side to side. The sun was small and bright in the sky; high up on the hunchback ridge a few rare cedars were growing. A swathe of soft sand extended along the river's left bank; the sand was white, the bodies lying on it dark and muscled – the soldiers were

talking, joking, smoking, not thinking about the fact that
tomorrow they would have to climb into the mountains once
more. It felt good. But towards evening Orshev started to have
sharp pains. It was an inflammation of the lungs and his
temperature shot up to 105°.

Orshev's comrades had already been home for a long time before
he was discharged from the medical unit. Thin and pale, Orshev
returned to his company. The bunks that had belonged to him
and his friends, the prestigious bunks on the lower tier, were
occupied by the old-timers who were now bosses in the
company. Orshev headed to the officers' quarters and found the
company commander. The captain talked straight with him,
allowed him to smoke right there in the office, poured him tea,
and got out some white bread and sugar. The captain said that
helicopters would be coming any day to bring more recruits and
that Orshev could fly back to Kabul when they arrived. But what
does 'any day' mean? It could be tomorrow or the day after, in a
week, in a fortnight. But then again, tomorrow morning a
column would be heading to Kabul for supplies. 'Of course,
driving to Kabul in a truck is risky business, you know that
yourself, Orshev. On the other hand it's tomorrow morning for
sure. Which means that you'd be in Kabul by evening, and the
next day, if you manage to catch a plane, in the Union. I'm not
recommending anything, you have to decide on your own.'
Orshev agreed to go. With a smile the captain handed him his
papers. 'So then, congratulations, your fighting's over.'

Orshev wandered through the little tent city flooded in steely
sunlight, and stood for a bit at the edge of the camp, smoking and
looking at the steppe, empty, silent, infinite. He should go to the
baths. But it was hot, and in any case his illness had softened his
firm body and Orshev felt lazy, weak, and flaccid. But he should

go anyway. Orshev plucked up his courage and headed for the battalion baths.

The plump attendant was sitting with a book on the front steps of the bathhouse. Orshev greeted him and asked if there was any water. 'We'll find some for you,' the attendant answered. Orshev sat down wearily beside him and admitted that he wasn't especially eager for a bath. 'Your eyes don't look too healthy, it's obvious they discharged you too soon,' the attendant said, slamming his book shut. 'When do you fly out?' Orshev answered that he'd be leaving with a column tomorrow. The attendant frowned in disapproval. 'I wouldn't go; it would be better to wait a month for a helicopter. Stay here and wait it out. You can sleep at my place, and tomorrow I'll be getting a ton of shit we can smoke. What do you say?' Orshev shook his head: he was tired, he was tired of hash, tired of everything.

He washed himself halfheartedly in tepid water, then dried himself; before getting dressed he carefully examined the seams of his fresh tee-shirt and shorts – often brand-new gear from the storehouse was already infested with fleas. While Orshev was busy in the baths the attendant brought a pot of water to boil on the fire behind the bathhouse and brewed some tea.

They sat on the steps, gulping tea, nibbling biscuits and sugar, looking at the little regimental town. The tents, the wood-planked mushrooms of the sentry-posts, the latrines, the dump, the mess-tents, headquarters, the storehouses, the officers' quarters, the parade grounds, the depots – everything looked grey from dust and sun.

Orshev sat until evening with the attendant and could have stayed there – the attendant slept in the bathhouse dressing-room – but Orshev wanted to spend his last night in his tent, which after all had been home for two years . . .

Orshev returned to his tent in the twilight and lay down on his bunk without undressing or turning back the sheets. The company was at nightly roll call and the tent was quiet. Orshev stared at the springs of the bunk above his and mulled over his condition with dissatisfaction. Something wasn't right, he felt; he wasn't really well yet. Or was it just the normal weakness one felt after being sick? Orshev dozed off.

He was woken up by a touch on his shoulder. He opened his eyes and saw an unfamiliar young soldier. The soldier was smiling in confusion. With his eyebrows and a light shake of the head Orshev asked: Well? 'I've been sent by the Soviet Army senior Khmyzin,' the young soldier muttered. Orshev said nothing. 'He,' the young soldier continued cautiously, 'asks that you give him his place back.' Orshev raised himself to his elbows and looked around: there were no old-timers, there was no Khmyzin in the tent, just youngsters, sparrows, and spooners. 'If he's so brave why hasn't he come to tell me himself?' Orshev asked sarcastically. 'That's your answer?' the young soldier asked. 'Go away,' Orshev said, but without anger. The youngster immediately left. But he returned quickly and said that the senior Khmyzin was warning him: once they finished smoking he had to get out. Orshev didn't reply. They're smoking, which means that they're all together, the jackals, Orshev thought. The youngster was waiting for an answer but didn't dare remind him. Orshev was lying back with his eyes closed. At last the old-timers came into the tent. Khmyzin, a stocky, squat, broad-chested young man, looked around at his comrades, walked determinedly up to Orshev's bunk, and said loudly: 'Orshev! Get out of my bunk!' Orshev opened his eyes and stared at Khmyzin. Khmyzin's comrades started to move. 'Stop, you jackals!' Orshev yelled, raising his hand imperiously. The old-timers froze. 'Khmyzin,' said Orshev, 'you want to flex your muscles, fine. But are you a man? Then speak for yourself. I always speak for myself.' 'That's fair enough,' one of the old-timers said at last. 'But he called us jackals,' another ventured uncertainly. No one answered him. But even if they had grudges against the ex-old-timers – Orshev and his comrades – in this quarrel they agreed, reluctantly, with Orshev. First of all, the worst of the ex-old-timers, the ones who deserved to be taught a lesson, had gone home long ago, and why should Orshev take a beating for everyone else? Second, there was nothing unnatural in the fact that they bore grudges against the ex-old-timers, no – as it was, so it will remain: yesterday they were abused, today they abuse. Third, beating the daylights out of a demob, a soldier who had been through hell and high water, would have set a bad example for the younger soldiers, who were now obeying their seniors as though they were gods – wise, powerful, bold. And for that matter Orshev had, all in all, never been that bad – he had kicked a few backsides and made others do all sorts of work for him, but he wasn't mean or rancorous and he had never come up with refined humiliations for the youngsters, sparrows, and spooners. And now the jackals had forgiven him and agreed that it was right: one against one. The old-timers drove everyone from the tent, cleared away all the little tables, scattered into the corners, and fixed their eyes on Khmyzin and Orshev. Orshev didn't have a belt on; someone told Khmyzin to take his off and he did. Everything became silent. And awkward. 'Come on, Khmyzin, let him have it!' someone cried out, and Khmyzin moved towards Orshev with his fists clenched and his head tucked in.

They closed in on each other. Khmyzin jerked his left shoulder to distract Orshev and with his right fist swung from the side and struck him in the temple. Orshev staggered and turned pale. Khmyzin swung towards his stomach but Orshev managed to deflect him. Khmyzin threw another roundhouse right with a straining grunt but Orshev parried that blow too. Orshev meanwhile had been on the defensive, coming back to his senses after the blow to his temple. Khmyzin attacked. He was now completely fearless, and his former indecision – how could he be fighting with an ex-old-timer, with someone he had never even dared look in the eye before – had vanished without a trace. Seeing that Orshev was doing little more than defending himself, Khmyzin flew into a rage and, grunting heatedly, started showering punches on his opponent. In his fervour Khmyzin grew careless and was astonished – everyone was astonished – when he found himself down on the ground. Khmyzin leaped up, shaking his head and spraying dark red drops, and Orshev immediately caught him under the eye with his left elbow and slammed his right fist into his cheek. Khmyzin gasped, bowed his head, shielded it with his hands, and started moving backwards. Orshev kept pressing him, landing heavy, accurate punches to his head, back, and kidneys. Everyone watched in silence. Suddenly Khmyzin stopped, bellowed, straightened up, and hurled himself on Orshev in an attempt to turn the fistfight into a wrestling match, but Orshev deftly stepped out of the way and struck Khmyzin in the nose. Khmyzin's lip was already split and now blood was flowing from his nose. The crazed Khmyzin again hurled himself on his opponent and this time managed to break through past his fists, clutch Orshev in his arms, and pull him down to the ground. Khmyzin found himself on top, grabbed Orshev by the hair, and started beating the back of his head against the floor; the pain brought tears to Orshev's eyes and he broke loose from Khmyzin, hammering him in the ribs with his fists. Everyone watched in silence. At last, covered in Khmyzin's blood, Orshev hit his opponent in the throat, and Khmyzin started wheezing and bit Orshev's hand. Orshev grabbed Khmyzin's ear with his other hand and tried to tear it off. Khmyzin screamed and let go of Orshev's hand, but Orshev kept twisting the ear and Khmyzin was forced to climb off him. Panting, Orshev raised himself on all fours. Khmyzin did too. They stood up slowly without taking their eyes off each other. 'You . . . had enough?' Orshev asked, and leaned against the back of the bunk. 'No . . . it's you . . . you . . . who's had enough,' answered Khmyzin, spitting out blood and wiping his nose on his sleeve. Orshev pushed himself off the back of the bunk, lashed his arm out, and struck Khmyzin in the neck with the edge of his hand. Khmyzin bowed his head again. Orshev stood up and waited. Khmyzin started, it seemed, to settle down. 'That's it,' Orshev said, but suddenly Khmyzin lunged towards him and smashed his forehead into Orshev's face. Orshev fell back against the bunk and clutched his nose, which was welling with blood; now both their noses were shattered. Stemming the blood with his hand, Orshev steadied himself against the bunk, looking at Khmyzin with dull eyes and holding his right arm at the ready: one more blow and he would go down. But Khmyzin didn't have the strength to attack; he was pouring sweat, wiping off blood, breathing drily and brokenly, reeling on unsteady legs.

'Looks as if that's it,' someone said in a loud voice. Orshev and Khmyzin kept their silence. 'Go and wash yourselves off,' they were advised. They dragged themselves outside the tent, and in the roadway young soldiers poured tins of water over them.

Orshev was the first to return to the tent; he pulled off his torn, bloodstained clothes and collapsed on the covers of his bunk.

Khmyzin came into the tent. He approached the disputed bed and said hoarsely, 'Orshev, get out of my place.' Everything fell silent in the tent. 'But it's my bunk,' Orshev answered after a few moments. 'Climb up into the upper row,' Khmyzin pronounced stubbornly, there's a bunk free there. I won't sleep up top anymore. Enough. A year and a half. Enough.' Orshev sat up.

'You're nothing, climb up onto the second level,' Khmyzin muttered. 'Go to hell,' Orshev said. 'Climb,' Khmyzin repeated. Orshev stood up and hit Khmyzin, but the blow fell short and landed on his chest. Khmyzin stepped back two paces, stumbled into a table, and caught his foot in it. 'Khmyzin!' the others yelled. Khmyzin didn't turn around at the shout; he stood half-facing Orshev so he could have more room for a swing and punch, but Orshev didn't wait: gripping the edge of the upper bunk in his curled hands, he hoisted himself up and kicked Khmyzin. Khmyzin flew backwards, landed between the bunks with a crash, and was still. Orshev collapsed onto his re-conquered bunk. 'Hey, you've killed him,' they were saying.

The orderly woke Orshev up at five in the morning: the column was heading out at six. 'How's the other one doing?' Orshev asked, yawning. 'He's sleeping,' the orderly replied. Orshev got up, stiff, grimacing, and went out into the road in his shorts and tee-shirt.

It was warm, birds were whistling; the bulbous red sun was lying on the edge of the steppe.

The orderly filled a pot with water from the barrel and poured it over Orshev. Orshev gingerly washed his aching face, nodded to the orderly and, carefully drying his face with a towel, went back into the tent. His dress uniform was hanging from the frame of the bunk – before he woke Orshev up the orderly had brought it from the store. Orshev dressed, picked up his case and cap, went to the middle of the tent and looked around. He spotted Khmyzin. He was asleep, his arms stretched out and his mouth wide open; there were dark bruises on his face, blood was caked around his nose, and his lower lip was split in half by a jagged black furrow. A small satisfied smile crossed Orshev's lips; he waved his cap at the sleeping Khmyzin and left the tent.

The commander of the column grinned when he saw Orshev's swollen face. 'So, party boy, had a good time?' Orshev answered that he was no party boy, he had just slept a lot at the medical unit. 'Yes of course,' the captain retorted, 'I'd guess what, little eagle, two, three litres? But anyway, where do you want to ride? A wheeled vehicle? A BTR? . . . A wheeled vehicle. Well, take your pick.'

Orshev walked the length of the column, stopped next to a truck, and asked the driver, 'Can you take me?' 'Get in,' the driver answered. In the cabin Orshev took off his jacket, hung it on the hook, asked for some water, drank it from the aluminium canteen, leaned his head against the back of the seat, and lit a cigarette.

Ten minutes later the column pulled out; at its head, tail, and middle went armoured transports with infantry aboard, the column guard. The column was slowly driving past the regimental CP. When Orshev's truck driver drew level with the little stone house, Orshev said to himself, 'Amen.'

The column picked up speed and started rolling along the steppe road, raising dust, rocking, rumbling. The sun was shining to one side, its rays piercing through the dust that shrouded the machines. Dust filtered into the cabin and stuck to one's eyes and lips, tickled one's nostrils, covered one's hair. The driver was calmly smoking a cigarette in the dust: its moistened end was already dirty. Orshev was bouncing a bit on the springy seat and staring at the blurry outline of the tarpaulin on the truck ahead of them. The driver was the quiet type, thank god, and had only been interested in why Orshev had stayed at the camp so long; he had said that in six months he would be going home too, and that was that. Orshev was content. After two years he was tired of these army conversations: about going home, about girls, about decorations, stripes, about good food. And anyway he had a splitting headache after the fight, as though he had really been drinking or smoking hash all night long.

Sometimes one of the vehicle's wheels hit a pothole and the driver and Orshev flew up from their seats. It was twenty miles from the camp to the first tarmac surface; the rebels liked to plant mines along this stretch, and the road looked like the surface of the moon. Vehicles could blow up on the tarmac too, but at least there was no dust there. It'll be paved road soon, Orshev was thinking.

The column travelled through clouds of dust on the steppe road for half an hour before it came to the tarmac and headed south along a straight grey road. Orshev took the bandage off his nose, rubbed his face, picked up the canteen, rinsed out his mouth, and drank. The driver lit a cigarette and said happily, 'It's nothing, just six months and I get out of here.' Orshev thought: six months which means twenty-four weeks, which means a hundred and eighty days – and his jaw tightened anxiously.

All around lay the steppes, with small, smoke-coloured heights and peaks rimming their edges. In the lifeless steppes were rare yellow *kishlaks*. Sometimes the *kishlaks* came right up to the surfaced road. They were gloomy collections of tumbledown buildings surrounded by high walls; houses, walls, wooden gates – everything was grey and primitive. The people – men in turbans, cloaks, and loose pantaloons, the women in dark shapeless gowns – would only rarely and timidly animate the sunlit little streets and gloomy squares. But behind the *duvals* was a mass of lush gardens, fresh, green, delicate gardens . . .

The column was moving swiftly. The mountains were coming closer, massive, reaching to the sky, reddening – the valley was becoming narrower. And soon the column was driving through the red and brown mountains. The road started to wind and rise up into the pass.

Orshev tossed a cigarette end out of the window and lit another; he was carefully watching the cliffs that towered up in either direction. Leaning forward, his brows knitted, the driver was turning the steering wheel and whistling, almost inaudibly, a monotonous little air. Orshev glanced sidelong at the sky and said, 'Hand me your assault rifle.' The driver shook his head: no way. Orshev smiled crookedly and by way of justifying himself said that not having an assault rifle was like not having an arm, and that he'd never gone anywhere without his. Gripping the wheel firmly in one hand, the driver fished out a pouch of grenades and handed it to Orshev. After a moment's hesitation he passed Orshev a second pouch too. Now Orshev had four grenades. He sighed with relief.

The column was climbing up a stone road pitted with craters. The cliffs were looming over the vehicles. The feet of the cliffs were black with scorchmarks. To the right yawned a precipice, not very deep, at whose bottom were charred wrecks, wheels, scraps of iron, shreds of rubber. The forward vehicles were already crawling through the saddle of the pass. Their engines were roaring, a pall of black smoke hung over the road, and the deep blue sky lay above the grey cliffs. Orshev was holding the pouches on his knees with one hand and smoking, and the driver was whistling his simple tune more and more loudly. And suddenly the vehicles ahead of them came to a halt one after the other until Orshev's driver had to brake too. 'Some idiot has broken down,' the driver ventured, and once more started whistling. Orshev took a sip from the canteen; the water was already warm. The driver was whistling and drumming his fingers on the steering wheel.

A minute passed. The column stayed where it was, engines humming in neutral. The driver was whistling and drumming. Orshev glanced down at the black scraps and debris. It was hot, hard to breathe, and beads of sweat were rolling down their faces. What the hell could have happened up ahead? One of the armoured transports must have overheated, common enough at the height of day in summer. Or one of the trucks' motors had died.

'Change the record, chief?' Orshev asked. The driver stopped whistling and drumming, closed his eyes, leaned back against the seat, and started breathing evenly and deeply, feigning sleep. Orshev smiled. I should have waited for a helicopter, he thought. I don't know what came over me to climb into that river, right now I could be . . . yes, home, a white shirt . . .

The engines roared to life and Orshev's driver opened his eyes and started whistling again. The column got going. Well, if nothing has happened so far, nothing's going to happen, thought Orshev, but then he corrected himself: In this pass.

The column made it through the pass and climbed downwards. The mountains receded a bit from the road. The sun was at its zenith, the slabs of stone on the mountains were glimmering as though made of glass, and the sky burned one's eyes. The driver put on teardrop-shaped sunglasses and looked as mysterious as a Sicilian mafioso. The rocky heights were sparkling, the roadside boulders were sparkling, and the truck's bonnet was burning. Orshev squinted, squinted, and fell asleep.

'They got one,' voices said loudly, and Orshev, startled, looked at the driver, who caught his eye and indicated off to the left with his head. The column was making its way around a few military vehicles with Afghan markings on their sides and a red and white passenger bus lying on its side in a ditch, its perforated undercarriage facing the road. Civilians and soldiers were crowding around the bus. There were no dead or wounded to be seen; they had probably been carted away already. A skinny, moustachioed soldier who looked like Don Quixote was pouring a canteen over his comrade's reddened hands. The pantaloons and cloaks on the civilians were torn and stained with fuel and blood. A bony old man was sitting apart from everyone else, his head buried in his knees, rocking back and forth. Also standing off to one side was a group of women in chadors. Two small, barefooted boys who had glanced at the column and lost interest in it were now trying to inspect the undercarriage of the bus – their heads were shoved into one of its gaps – but a grey-haired soldier started yelling at them. The Afghanis stared at the column.

The truck Orshev was riding in dropped down into the ditch, drove parallel to the road for a while, then returned to the tarmac. The driver started whistling. Orshev looked at his watch and asked, 'Listen, do you stop for lunch or eat it on the road?'

'We stop. We'll be coming to a river soon, that's where we usually stop for grub.'

'Mmm. The thing is I haven't eaten since yesterday.'

'So eat, what's the matter with you? What, you haven't got anything to eat?'

'I have. But I don't want to eat alone.'

'Forget it, get it down you.'

'No, not alone, I'll wait for a while.'

Orshev was rocked to sleep again and woke up when the column came to a stop in front of a bridge. Two engineers and an Alsatian were already roving around the bridge. The other soldiers were smoking, wandering around the vehicles, throwing off their sweat-stiff jackets, and jumping into the river to wash themselves; Orshev and the driver went too. They came back to the vehicle refreshed, left its doors wide open, and laid out their food: black bread, sugar, two cans of stewed lamb, and two cans of cheese. They ate in silence. First they ate the meat with the sour bread, then the sugar and cheese. They drank some water,

lit cigarettes, and far away on the steppe they sighted a caravan –
a line of camels, little silhouettes of people walking, white sheep.
'Ah, Pathans,' the driver said lazily, then yawned. 'No bullshit for
them, war or no war they just roam around.'

'Gypsies,' responded Orshev.

'We had a gypsy once' – the driver stirred – 'But all the same,
a gypsy's a gypsy: black, big-eyed, cunning. We went down to
Kabul once. They made us take a bath at the pass. Afterwards the
gypsy got sick. He was in the medical unit, then in Kabul, and
from there to the Union, and we never saw him again.'

'What was the matter with him?'

'Something like his liver. Or his stomach. They say he was a
tobacco addict. But what an idea to come up with – a gypsy in the
army.'

'So, he wasn't the type?'

'Of course not. A gypsy would be a gypsy even in Africa – give
him a whip, a horse, and the wind. All he gets here is the whip. I
like them.'

Orshev didn't understand: 'Who?'

'Gypsies, of course. They don't care about anything. A horse, a
whip, and the wind. And we're the donkeys.' The driver stared
ruefully at the steppe, where, at the base of the bare mountains,
tiny camels and thin silhouettes of people were moving along
amid the soft white fleece of sheep.

Kabul was lit by an evening sun, viscous, hot, swollen, and
murky, that was resting on the snow-covered peaks. The city lay
in a mountainous valley, a huge city of earth, stone, glass, and
tarmac; fluffy gardens and tall, conical poplars everywhere;
among the gardens, the glittering windows, and the white walls
were the blue cupolas of mosques and soaring yellow minarets.

The column halted at a fenced-in site at the edge of the city.

Orshev put on his jacket and cap, picked up his case, and turned to the driver. His heavy hands on the wheel, the driver looked at Orshev. 'Well,' Orshev said, then paused. 'Until we meet in the Union?' He held his hand out to the driver. The driver took his hand limply and answered that it was unlikely they'd meet again; the Union was pretty big. 'Six months is nothing,' Orshev said, and climbed down from the cabin.

He found the captain and asked him if they'd take him to the transit camp. 'Ah, listen, our chauffeur is exhausted, why don't you wait until tomorrow morning,' the captain said merrily. 'Where are you racing off to? No more planes are flying and there are fleas at the camp. Spend the night with us. I'll tell you a bedtime story about the White Ox. What, you don't want me to?' The captain burst out laughing. Orshev was staring sullenly at him, not saying anything, when an aircraft started to drone in the sky over Kabul. The captain, the infantrymen, and Orshev looked up. In the sky, soaring, gaining altitude, was a white aircraft with a purple stripe from its nose to its tail. 'Oh! Look! Your plane's gone bye-bye!' the captain exclaimed with a laugh.

'It isn't one of ours,' one of the infantrymen objected, 'ours are white and blue.'

'But a new order came down that ours have to have a red stripe, didn't you hear? Well, brothers, you're out of touch,' the captain said. The infantrymen were puzzled: what, was it true? 'And how. Listen: is our flag red? A Pioneer tie? A passport? Service papers? Hmm? So why should our planes be white and blue? There they are, flying overseas, with no ideological content, no ideological content at all in their colouring. How could that be? Either an oversight or provocation.' The captain looked at Orshev. 'Oh! Oh! The demob's going to rip me apart now, ha-ha-ha!'

'Comrade captain,' Orshev said, then shut up.

'But admit it, if I didn't have my stripe – no, my stripes – you'd hit me now, wouldn't you?' the captain asked. 'Ha-ha-ha! Come on – watch it – honestly now. Wouldn't you?' The infantrymen and the armoured transport driver started to mutter peevishly, comrade captain, come on the bloke should really be given a lift.

'You would, oh, but how you would,' the captain said, 'I can see it in your eyes. I'd guess you wiped out a pile of *doukh*s, little eagle? But! Okay, okay, I'm only joking. Stop sulking, we'll get you there. We'll get you there safe and sound. Corporal, come here!'

Orshev, four infantrymen, and the corporal climbed onto an armoured transport and headed towards the city. Orshev's eyes picked out the quiet driver's truck and he waved his hand at him – the driver was sitting and smoking in the cabin. 'You should sit below,' the corporal called out to Orshev. 'Don't tempt fate – snipers!' Orshev shook his head. 'Fine, fine,' the corporal said, casting a benevolent look at Orshev.

Rocking gently, the green armoured transport was sailing along a wide main road lined with poplars and cedars. Passenger cars, buses, trucks, and cyclists were driving along the main road. The sides of the road were packed with *karachival*s – ragged-looking men with two-wheeled wooden push-carts loaded with bags, packs, and firewood: delivery vans for the poor. People were walking along the pavements: old men with white beards in relief against black European coats, officers and soldiers with assault rifles, bushy-haired youths in colourful shirts, jeans, and pants, dirt-caked naked children, women in chadors, and white-faced, black-haired girls in short denim skirts and light blouses. *Dukan*s were screaming out their wares, store windows and restaurant signs were sparkling, shashlik was being grilled in the street, stray dogs were howling, children twittering, engines roaring, brakes squealing, the evening wind was stirring the poplar and plane-tree leaves, and high above the city the mountaintops were glowing red with the sun disappearing behind them.

The transit station, a tent camp surrounded by barbed wire, was on the other side of the city, not far from the airport. The night was still light when the armoured transport stopped in front of the camp gates. Orshev said good-bye to the infantrymen and corporal and jumped to the ground. A sentry appeared at the gates.

Orshev didn't sleep but lay on his bare bunk, his case thrust under his head, smoking and staring at the ceiling. The recruits – the camp was full of them – were breathing and snoring in boyish concert. Orshev wasn't feeling good, his head was aching, the hand Khmyzin had bitten was throbbing, and it seemed that his temperature had gone up. Orshev was thinking: not well yet. He smoked and glanced at the glowing dial on his watch – time wasn't rushing by.

At one in the morning a bang broke the silence, then a shout and an explosion could be heard. A moment later there was the jerk of another, closer this time, and shrapnel whistled over the tents. The camp defences opened fire with assault rifles and machine-guns. The recruits were leaping up and screaming at one another: Where? What? Alert! What was that? They leaned out of their tents and saw black mountains and red tracer bursts. 'They're bombarding us, they're bombarding us!' they had all begun yelling when a third shell exploded close by, somewhere beyond the barbed wire. Orshev was lying down, smoking and thinking that this is how it would be, he had imagined it happening like this, at the very last curtain call.

'Are those shells?' they asked him. Orshev answered yes. The new recruits were crowding around the door and looking out of the windows. Orshev suddenly saw it all very clearly: there they are in the blackness, one of them is shoving a cylinder with metallic feathers on its tail into the muzzle, leaping back, and the mortar hurls the cylinder – whistling gently, hypnotically, it rushes through the night and ploughs into the top of the tent. Orshev could hear and see the recruits writhing, rolling, struggling to get out, choking, moaning, screaming, not believing that this could be happening on their very first day, and Orshev saw himself clutching a wet, burning, sticky hole in his stomach – now . . .

But the mortar wasn't firing any more. The defences were pouring bursts into the mountains. In half an hour everything was quiet. The camp was stirring, talking, lighting cigarettes; no more shouts could be heard, which meant that all the shells had fallen away into the bracken. Orshev smoked another cigarette and, lulled by the talking of the recruits, fell asleep. In his sleep he thought: the weather will be good, there will be an aeroplane, the weather will be good and there will be a plane, weather, plane.

The weather was good and there was a plane. It was a transport craft from Bagram, loaded with coffins and their escorts, that was picking something else up in Kabul. Orshev found out that the first stop would be Orenburg, then Minsk and Moscow. That was fortunate. Demobilized soldiers were usually brought to Tashkent, from where it was left entirely up to them to get home – no problem in the winter, but in summertime, when the train station and airport were overcrowded, one was forced to loiter around in Tashkent for days. Orshev, who had to go to Moscow and then further west, was in serious luck.

Orshev settled himself on a folding seat in the tail section. It was stuffy. He ditched his jacket, pulled off his tie, unbuttoned his shirt.

The sombre soldiers, in ironed and spotless field uniforms with snow-white undercollars, were looking at him sullenly – they had to deliver the coffins home and say a few words at the funerals and memorial suppers. Among the escort were two officers, so there were officers in the coffins too. Long, matt metal coffins, roughly welded in the middle, were sitting two-by-two in the aircraft. The officers were talking about this and that. The soldiers were silent.

At last the pilots in their light blue suits entered the aircraft. The plane's tail doors shut tightly, it became murky, and the ceiling lights up above began to glow dully. The aircraft engines whined and it started moving, taxied to the runway, picked up speed, and took off. Those sitting by the few portholes pressed their heads against the thick glass. Orshev wanted to see Kabul one last time, but going up to someone and asking him to move aside for a minute – no, he couldn't go up and ask anyone. Orshev looked at the soldiers, at the metallic boxes, at the ceiling, at his feet . . . He closed his eyes.

The aircraft struggled to gain altitude. It was hot. Sweat was running down their faces. Orshev wanted to smoke. He hadn't smoked in ages – while the transport was being loaded he had sat for an hour under the shade of its wings, but smoking wasn't allowed on the airfield. There was a weakness in his body. When he took a deep breath he felt an ache in his back around the top of the left lung. Or was that his heart? No, his heart was healthy, it had been quiet for two years, so it was working fine, even though they had run up and down the mountains like horses. No, it was his lungs. He hadn't been treated long enough, that was all. Or maybe Khmyzin had landed a good one there, that was why it ached. But this damn weakness . . .

How long to the border – half an hour, an hour? Orshev was thinking. It's too early to cheer until we cross the border. But we've reached a decent altitude, they couldn't get us now, we're out of range. So – Hip hip! Hip hip!

The Yellow Mountain

It was dry, warm, yellow. His body was light. A strange woman growing out of the earth was feeding him red berries from her hand. A downy white lump was pressing against his cheek, a warm, heavy lump.

And there was an explosion.

Pryadilnikov screamed and woke up. He sat up in his bed, rubbed his eyes, looked around, and realized that he had been asleep in his tiny apartment and that the ringing of his alarm clock had woken him. He stretched, set his feet down on the floor, walked towards the table, and switched on the tape deck. In the mornings he listened to rock. And this morning he listened to rock. It was invigorating, like strong Indian tea or rich Brazilian coffee. Pryadilnikov opened the blinds. The street was sunny. It was a warm, early Russian autumn.

Pryadilnikov walked barefoot to the toilet, then to the sink. After washing he went into the kitchen, took three eggs out of the refrigerator, turned the gas on under the tea kettle and frying-pan. When the frying-pan was hot he dropped a bit of butter into it; the butter melted quickly, and into the yellow, foamy little pool he slipped three eggs, convex, white and yellow, covered with a transparent slime.

In nothing more than his underpants Pryadilnikov sat down at the table, ate the fried eggs and three slices of bread with butter, and drank two cups of bitter, ruby-coloured tea. After breakfast he returned to his bedroom, grabbed an ashtray, matches, and cigarettes, lay down on the bed, struck a match, lit a cigarette.

Dove-coloured locks and curls snaked down over his face.

The rock was rocking: Hey, come along with us, with us everything is simple, black is black, white is white, it's better to be lying back in a clearing with your girl and a can of beer than to play the games of adult idiots, it's better to be poor but tell lies to nobody, submit to nobody, give orders to nobody, we're telling you to love yourself, your girl, your beer, and to stop nobody else from doing the same thing, it's better than preaching about love for all humanity, demanding everyone love one another without loving themselves, to put ideals and duty far above everything else — it's better than preaching, demanding, forcing, and time after time committing massacre for the sake of the triumph of your humanitarian ideals, you can't believe, no, can't believe anyone, anytime, anything, my friend, you can't believe.

The nicotine and the rock were dissolving in his blood, and Pryadilnikov was high.

You can't believe, no, can't believe . . .

His mood was just fine. It wasn't good very often. Such a swollen head all the time — everything was always wrong, but today everything was all right. But why?

Had he dreamed something, perhaps?

Yes, it seemed he had.

Have to remember — but later, later. For now, rock.

Pryadilnikov looked at his watch. It was time. He got up, put on jeans, a black sweater, and light suede shoes. He glanced into the mirror. Not too bad. Healthier-looking. Limping, Pryadilnikov left the apartment.

His 'armoured car', a Zaporozhets the colour of sand was parked near the entryway. Pryadilnikov wiped the fogged windscreen with a rag, got in, turned the key in the ignition, warmed the engine up, put the car into gear, and set out. The armoured car wound through stone labyrinths, reached a broad street, and started gliding past bus stops and crowds, shops and restaurants. Pryadilnikov switched on the radio, twisted the tuning knob, and came across some rock. The rock was still rocking the same thing: if the pot-bellied men in top hats haven't already led you astray with their speeches and slogans, come to us, we're not going anywhere since there's nowhere to go, and we won't tell lies about going somewhere and getting there in the end, we're just marking time, and we don't give a damn who you are – red or black, left or right, Christian or Buddhist, atheist or anarchist – you're a human being, that's enough, that's all there is to say, you'll come to us because you're sick of humanitarian fables written in your blood and mine, let them smash one another's top hats and heads in, but we'll be looking at the sun, kissing our girls, and listening to rock, rock has united us, our ideology and our religion is rock.

That's great, Pryadilnikov thought, only naive, kids. Those gentlemen in their top hats will suddenly start swearing, calling each other names, and send you your orders. And there won't be anywhere for you to run, you'll go off to defend the honour of those top hats, and you'll disembowel your brothers in rock.

He drove into the carpark, thinking that he didn't really have to come here today, parked his car among the black and grey Volgas, and started limping towards the main entrance of the columned building. I shouldn't have come here, he thought again.

Sober-looking men in suits and ties were going into the

edifice, nodding curtly and offering each other their soft white hands; women were going into the building too, all of them dressed the same way – *à la* Iron Lady of London.

On the fourth floor of the columned building, under the wings and the indefatigable eyes of the district powers, were the editorial offices of two newspapers, one for the Party, the other for youth. It was in the latter that the lame, chain-smoking, sickly young man named Pryadilnikov was an employee. He had been coming to this building every morning for a year now. He should have got used to it. But he wasn't used to it at all. And this morning, finding himself in the spacious reception area with its mirrors, its shoe-polishing machine, and its two militiamen behind a small table covered with black and white telephones, Pryadilnikov felt awkward, like an uninvited guest at a party, a party filled with complete strangers. He walked past the militiamen and looked the other way. He had never learned how to nod to them baronially, and fraternally – he couldn't do it.

There were two lifts, one to carry up those whose offices were in the right wing, the other for the left-wing workers. He had to take the left one, but among the left-wingers he spotted a familiar round face and he swung to the right. Ah, him, that Zavsepech. A total bore. He was the director of the press section, and every newspaper in the district was under his control. He had started out as the Party secretary at the 'Twenty Years Without a Harvest' kolkhoz, or something to that effect. Now he was the Zavsepech.

Once, on the eve of Red Army Day, the Zavsepech had proposed that Pryadilnikov say a few words at the ceremonial assembly. Pryadilnikov had declined: I don't speak well, I don't know what to say, no. The Zavsepech started coaching him about what was needed and how it was accomplished, and he got carried away: Our people have lived so long under peaceful skies, but you, on your generation it befell . . . um, um . . . it befalls . . . it befell, that is, circumstances were such that your . . . you were called by international duty to defend, guns in hand, the nascent revolution of our fraternal brother to the south, and there you rendered that help, couldn't you come with your medal so we can admire it and know that our successors will be worthy successors, traditions, internationalism, Spain, heroes of the revolution, the southern borders, the Americans weren't dozing, where there's trouble they're in like that – zap! – but you wouldn't let those falcons and hawks rip the young revolution to shreds, terror, bandits, intrigues, bravery, honour, Russian arms, to sunny days – yes! yes! yes! – to nuclear explosions – no! no! no!

'My medal's being repaired,' Pryadilnikov had said. His editor shook his fist at him behind the Zavsepech's back. The Zavsepech was taken by surprise: 'How's that?' The editorial office had fallen joyously silent. Behind the Zavsepech, the editor was making terrifying faces. 'The fronting fell off,' Pryadilnikov said. 'I've been wearing it around a lot.' The editor cut in: 'You'll speak without the medal. He'll speak, Demyan Vasilevich.'

But on the following day Pryadilnikov wheedled a job out of his supervisor, the department head, and disappeared for the day. From that time on the Zavsepech would stop Pryadilnikov whenever they ran into each other, clap him on the shoulder, and say, 'Young man, it seems to me that you don't quite understand something; of course, you did take, as they say, an immediate part in it, but from the trenches you can only see one side of the fighting, and even if you could see every side of every battle it isn't enough, because apart from the visible battles there are the hidden ones, imperceptible to a superficial glance, there are complexities inaccessible to superficial thinking . . .'

Pryadilnikov went into the lift with two women and a grey-

haired man. The lift started to rise. The man looked disapprov-
ingly at the journalist's well-worn jeans and was probably
regretting that it was only women who were forbidden from
coming here in capitalistic trousers. Pryadilnikov eyed the
women in their severe suits. Dry water. Crooked straight line.
Sweet lemon. But they're perfect for it, just perfect, he thought,
looking at the woman officials. And it would be even more
perfect if all the men were thrown the hell out of the building.
The men were pretty much just dead weight. But these women,
shit.

He got out on his floor and started limping along the crimson-
carpeted corridors to the left wing. When he passed by the door
with OBLLIT written on it he recalled how the second page of
the youth newspaper had once been blocked out. In one sentence
in a small article of literary criticism, the names of a well-known
writer and Bulgakov had both appeared. The editor was
telephoned and told that linking the well-known Soviet writer
and Bulgakov in the same commendatory sentence was nonsense.
The editor was an easy-going person. But sometimes his
emotions got the better of him. He'll be working away, working
away, not saying anything, doing what he's told, and suddenly
he'll spot the latest red-calico watchword – 'Trampling on
headgear is strictly prohibited!' – and he'll tear off his shabby cap
and start jumping up and down on it. And this time too his
emotions got him. The editor replied that he, the whole editorial
office, the author of the article, and intelligent people all over the
planet saw no nonsense in it at all. But the person he had by
implication ranked among the world's unintelligent people was
beside himself and answered the following: Praising Whites plays
into the hands of the enemy, malevolent nostalgia, decadent
tone, the universal aims of Socialist Realism, a corrupting
influence on developing hearts and minds, a perverted represen-

tation of reality, we, the Soviet people, who sense the greatness of the everyday, we declare a decisive no! This lackey, this slanderer, cannot stand beside a great Soviet writer!

But the editor was having none of it: 'Then the newspaper won't run. The whole issue.' 'What? What is this? Sabotage?' 'In a nutshell, yes,' the editor replied, and hung up. Five minutes later he was summoned to the Chief Censor of OBLLIT. He heard the editor out and recommended resolving the question by having one writer appear in one sentence and the other in another. Solomon.

The student youth department was already smoky and smelling of coffee. The department director started clapping: 'Oh! Fedya didn't drink last night either!'

'He must have run out of money,' suggested the department's bearded correspondent, who was handsome and sad-looking.

'Fedya, come over here,' the department director called out.

Pryadilnikov walked over to her desk; she set her cigarette down on the edge of an ashtray, got up, firmly gripped his neck in her hand, pulled his head towards her, and kissed him on the lips. 'Encore,' the bearded man said.

The other correspondent, just graduated from Moscow State University, a petite girl with big hazel eyes and curly hair, blushed and turned away.

'Okay, I won't do it anymore or Marina will end up pouring poison in my coffee,' the director said, letting go of Pryadilnikov.

'Hah!' the young journalist said.

Pryadilnikov sat down at his desk.

'Marina, why don't you give him some coffee,' the director said, then picked up her cigarette and pulled on it.

'You want some?' the petite journalist asked, looking at Pryadilnikov warmly. He nodded.

The girl stood up, gracefully walked over to the bookcase,

picked up the pot of coffee, soundlessly and smoothly poured the brown liquid into a large cup, and brought it to Pryadilnikov. He thanked her, took the cup, and his large fingers brushed against her small ones. The director, a woman in her thirties who had already started the struggle against common sense and time, smiled thinly – her smiles had been infrequent and thin for some time, so the wrinkles would be smaller. The bearded man smiled too, but dreamily: What nice little legs.

'Fedya, is it true that you haven't got any money?' the director asked.

'I have, I have,' Pryadilnikov replied, and sipped his coffee. 'I've just decided to be an angel.'

'I'll give you some, don't be shy,' the director said.

'She'll give it to you, don't doubt it,' the cartoonist and caricaturist Gostyev said as he came into the room. 'Will you give it to me too, Louisa?'

Louisa – Liza, the director – was unfazed and answered, 'And you only have one thing on your mind.'

'Yup. Freud said that it's on everyone's mind all the time.'

'I wonder what's on the chief's mind today. Have you seen him? Which side of the bed was he good enough to get out on?'

Gostyev was about to say something about the editor and his bed, but he didn't have the chance. The door opened and, puffing on a cheap cigarette, into the room came the editor, an imposing, big-eared man in glasses.

'Yegor Petrovich!' exclaimed Gostyev, standing at attention and thrusting out his chest. 'Companee! Atten-shun!'

'Get out of here,' the editor said, his large, tobacco-stained teeth showing when he smiled.

'Yessir!' Gostyev walked out in ceremonial step but immediately returned. 'Permission to stand guard here!' he exclaimed by the door.

'Numskull,' the editor said.

'Thank you, sir!'

'Good morning, Yegor,' said the director.

The editor had passed the maximum Komsomol age limit ten years before, but he thought of himself as young and insisted on being called nothing more than Yegor, although, of course, only if there were no outsiders around.

'Morning,' the editor replied. 'You drinking coffee?'

'Coffee for the editor!' Gostyev bellowed, and rushed off to the bookcase to pour some into the editor's oversized baked-clay cup.

The editor chuckled and sat down on a free stool.

'So, Fedya, why are you looking so sad behind those deep blue pools?' the editor asked Pryadilnikov with a smile. He always asked the question if he had woken up on the good side of his bed. He had borrowed the 'deep blue pools' from Yesenin, his favourite poet.

'Fedya's looking well today,' the director said.

'Is he?' The editor looked him over. 'What, no money? But I won't give you any, so don't even ask. If you turned your empties in you'd have enough for food. Get yourself dried out.'

'He needs to get married,' the editor said, her eyes moving in the direction of Marina.

'Let's get him a wife,' the editor said resolutely.

'Fast as we can,' the Beard sighed. His own wife ran off to her mother's when he came home drunk and couldn't convince her that he had good reason to be so.

Their tongues thoroughly stretched, the journalists took up their pens.

Pryadilnikov was working on an article about military and patriotic instruction in the city schools. Pryadilnikov wrote. Marina glanced at him every now and then from the side. The

Beard had left to interview someone. The director was looking for a book in the bookcase.

Pryadilnikov ran the tip of his pen across a piece of paper, and a flock of birds was slowly landing on the steppe before bare, soft hills; he and the other guards watched silently while the large black birds with small heads floated down towards the grass and flowers; it was early in the morning, quiet, the company was asleep in its armoured transports; the birds were landing, folding their huge wings, cleaning their feathers with their beaks, looking around, wandering through the flowers; they had white stripes running from their beaks to their breasts and red crowns on their heads, and every so often they would stand still, turn their heads towards the column, and stare at it; the guards didn't budge and the birds probably mistook them for pillars, and the armoured transports for shining green turtles; the white-necked birds were striding back and forth on the steppe, the birds were black, the steppe green, the bare hills and the herd of green turtles were asleep, there was already a crimson light in the sky to the east, and it was quiet, warm . . .

The door opened.

'I won't even give this to OBLLIT, Fyodor,' the editor said, walking in and handing a manuscript to Pryadilnikov. 'They'll tear it to pieces.'

'That's what I thought too,' Pryadilnikov replied.

'You understand . . .'

'I understand that I'm not really Soviet, I suppose.'

'Come on, don't generalize. And don't take it to heart. That's all. And you know that for now you can write for the desk drawer. Sometime, perhaps . . . umm. But right now – alas!'

'Understood.'

'And something else. You know, everything somehow turns

out to be so subjective with you. Was it all really so gloomy? Nothing but negatives, hmm?'

'No, not at all. They gave us free cigarettes. You didn't have to shave during operations. Well actually you did, but the officers didn't look too closely at your stubble. What else? They shipped us vodka from the Union in tanker trucks.'

'Ha-ha.' The editor laughed humourlessly.

'Thirty coupons per bottle. But you could steal boots, petrol, or heating fuel for the *dukan*s and get enough to buy a bottle.'

'Negatives, sheer negatives. A journalist has to be objective. In every article there has to be both negative and positive. That's what objectivity means.'

'I can't. I'm blunt, unihemispherical.'

'Why's that?'

'Only one hemisphere works, the pessimistic one; the optimistic one burst from dyspepsia.'

'Don't talk nonsense. And do try to be objective. Try, Fyodor,' the editor said, then left.

'Memoirs?' the director asked coldly. She wasn't pleased that Pryadilnikov had given the manuscript to the editor and not to her.

'Yes, memoirs. And nothing to do with what our department does,' Pryadilnikov said.

The director was silent.

'Fedya,' Marina called out to him. 'Can I read them please?'

'It's garbage.'

'Come on, Fedya.'

He shrugged his shoulders and handed her the manuscript.

*

AN ARMY ORATORIO

His name was Akimov. At the time in question he was a major, the regimental chief of staff. A stocky major of medium height with hard eyes, small hands, and boots that were always shiny. Close-shaven. Not a speck of dust on his uniform although the place was dusty – in summer djinns of dust would dance on the steppe around the camp, from time to time they would band together and fall on it with a roar, and the sky would grow dark, the sun would go dim, and a biblical haze would shroud our small tent city.

We four soldiers were assigned to the guard of the regimental CP. It was a long posting; it lasted five months. The command thought it more expedient to have a permanent guard for the regimental CP. And in fact it was better than rotating personnel who would carry out their duties in a less than meticulous way. So we, the permanent guard, prized the life we were leading without the incessant surveillance of officers, training, drills, and route marches, and we performed our duties avidly. Everyone called the CP 'the village' and envied us. The small stone house, actually more of a hut, stood a kilometre away from the camp on a road that led off into the steppe; this road and another road on the opposite side of the camp were the only unmined stretches of land – the camp was entirely surrounded by minefields, and the roads linked the camp to an alien, hostile world.

We watched the road around the clock. Two would sleep while two, in flak jackets, would be on guard. We had our meals with the battalion. Still, we did have, of course, a fireplace in a dugout, a tea kettle, and a bowl for pilafs. On the walls hung pictures cut out from magazines, there were books on the table, and we had a short-wave radio hidden away. There was a home-made pack of cards. We didn't live badly.

Every night the duty officer would call on us, or sometimes the chief of staff Akimov or the camp Zampolit.

Akimov loved Blok. The poet. Aleksandr Blok.

He looked in once to make sure that we hadn't been drinking liquor or smoking hash. We hadn't been smoking or drinking, and everything was in order, even our undercollars were clean. The major was still satisfied with us. He spotted a little volume of Blok's poems on the table, asked whose book it was; I said I had borrowed it from the library, and he recited, in a melancholy voice, 'At night, above the restaurants,' said that he was his favourite poet, took the little volume, and allowed me to come to see him in a week's time. A week later I went to camp and waited an hour for the major at headquarters; he appeared, invited me into his office, held the book out to me, and said: Poems of crystal. I answered: Yes, not steel. He looked at me closely. I broke into a sweat. Well, off you go, he said, and dismissed me.

Major Akimov put an end to our life at 'the village'.

It was evening. Snow was falling. We were stoking the stove. One man in a canvas cloak was pacing back and forth in front of the barricade in the road; sometimes he walked up to the window and looked in at us. It was hot, smoky, and noisy inside. We were baking flatcakes and roasting potatoes. We were celebrating someone's birthday. A shy young boy, he was sitting, his arms folded, waiting for the presents and guests. The guests soon arrived. There were two of them, and they brought half a tin of condensed milk and a pair of braces: braces were all the rage with us.

We sat down at the table, grapefruit juice was poured into our cups, and I was getting up to make a speech when the sentry rapped on the snow-crusted window and said: A car! Everyone was suddenly terrified and started stashing the food under the bed, and the guests hurled themselves outside. I tried to stop them and said: But what's all this for if we're just celebrating a birthday? But no one heard me.

The car pulled up. We waited. A car door slammed. The muffled voice of our sentry could be heard reporting that since he had come on guard – and so on. The door opened and into the little house came Major Akimov, glowering, and the regimental duty officer, a lieutenant. Akimov looked around at our sweaty, cowering faces. From under the bed came the smell of flatcakes and potatoes, and on the table lay bread, jam, and a pile of sliced large onions.

'Get it out,' Akimov said, 'everything.'

We pulled the frying pan and the plate of cakes out from under the bed.

'I said everything,' Akimov prodded.

'That is everything,' our sergeant said.

'The liquor!'

We shrugged our shoulders.

'Lieutenant,' Akimov called out.

The lieutenant rummaged through everything, looked under the pillow, then went outside.

'Comrade major,' our sergeant began to explain, 'we have a birthday . . .'

The lieutenant returned with the two snow-covered guests.

'They were lying down in the trench.'

'So,' the major said, becoming animated. He took off his cap, smoothed his hair, and sat down at the little table.

'Where do you come from?' the lieutenant asked the guests. They fidgeted, hung their heads dejectedly, and said nothing.

'Where do you come from?' the major asked quietly, and the guests sighed, raised their heads, and stated their names and units.

'Unauthorized personnel are not allowed at the CP, do you know that?' the lieutenant asked.

The guests said nothing.

'Do you know that?' the major asked, and the guests answered in chorus: Absolutely! Not at all!

One knew, the other didn't.

'So,' the major said. 'You don't know either, sergeant?'

'Yes, but it's a birthday,' our sergeant said, 'and we're on permanent detachment . . .'

'Permanent?' The major turned white. 'Parasites,' he said quietly.

He glanced at the table and suddenly struck the handle of the pan with the edge of his palm. The potatoes fell to the ground.

'A birthday party,' the major said through his teeth, and stood up. 'A birthday party! They're having a birthday party! Enemies all around just longing to cut everyone's throats! It's war, I tell you! And they're having a birthday party. A birth . . . Why are you still sitting down?'

The boy whose birthday it was leaped up off the bed and stood to attention.

'They're stuffing themselves, making pigs of themselves! Permanent detachment! I'll show you permanent . . . I'll teach you . . . mothers . . . The whole camp in zinc-lined boxes? In zinc, eh? . . . They're having a birthday party! Yes, lieutenant, just look, just look at these badgers in their hole! Permanent detachment!'

Someone giggled, I don't remember who. No doubt from nervousness. But it was enough to make the chief of staff's eyes jump entirely from their sockets.

'Funny? You think it's funny?'

He grabbed the loaf of bread, heavy and brown, and swept the cans, the salt, the flatcakes, the cups off the table. Terrified, one of the guests threw himself outside; the lieutenant sprang out after him and dragged him back. He was holding him by the ear: What were you doing, eh? What were you going to do? Where were you going? To the *doukhs*, maybe?

The soldier started crying. The major turned even whiter and frowned in disgust.

'Get rid of it all! Now!'

I grabbed a broom to sweep up the potatoes, flat cakes, salt.

'With your hands,' the major said. 'Your hands. Hands! Come on!'

I stood there with my head bowed. My legs were trembling.

'Come on!'

I don't know. Maybe I bent down and started to pick the food up with my hands. I don't know. I'm something of a coward. But I didn't have time to make a complete coward of myself because our sergeant suddenly tried something on. He strode over towards the pyramid of assault rifles and muttered, distinctly: 'We're in a combat post.'

The oven singing. Snow outside the window. Silence.

The major glanced at the lieutenant.

'Whoa!' the lieutenant said and walked towards the sergeant.

The major burst out laughing. 'The movies! No, you won't die of boredom.' He stopped laughing. 'Fine. Everyone will go to the cooler. The sentries for seven days, the guests for three. And you,' he said to the sergeant, 'but you I . . .'

'Give him to Zhilmurdayev,' the lieutenant suggested, 'he likes hotheads like him.'

Zhilmurdayev was the commander of the infantry battalion's third company, and 'difficult cases' were sent to him for reeducation. The 'difficult cases' quickly turned tractable.

The major suddenly said: 'No. But you I congratulate.'

No doubt the major thought himself a second Suvorov.

From that time there was a daily change of guard at the CP. Our 'village' life came to an end. But that's beside the point.

In the summer a young soldier ran away from camp. For three days and nights soldiers scoured the steppes and *kishlak*s, but they never caught the deserter. The matter drew some attention and an inquiry was launched. It became clear that the veterans . . . well, too many horrors, bestial, all kinds of inhumanities, and representatives of high command flew into camp. After investigating the matter they resolved to punish the guilty parties severely. Before returning to Kabul the officers called together the Komsomol activists from every unit for a discussion. My company sent me, although never in my whole life have I been an activist, especially not in the army – it was simply my idiotic habit at any gathering to ask the officers questions that would entertain a bored audience, and the officers considered me an activist.

The discussion took place in the regimental club. The club had neither walls nor a ceiling; there were rows of wooden benches, a semi-circular stage, a huge, concave white screen, sky and sun. On the stage were tables, and behind the tables sat majors and colonels in field uniforms: thick, distinguished moustaches, Roman chins, spectacles in thin frames, penetrating eyes, taut, close-shaven cheeks, snow-white undercollars, strong bald heads, and brows glistening with sweat.

The first to stand up was the commander of our regiment, Major Akimov. He said: A peaceful foreign policy, but when things go badly for our neighbours we step in, tense days, imperialist machinations, undeclared war, losses, hardships, the glorious Armed Forces, trials by fire, traditions, great martial spirit, patriotism, superb military and political preparation, scores of successful operations, Orders of the Red Star, scores of decorations, three Heroes . . . Akimov poured some water out of the decanter into his glass and swallowed it in one gulp as though it were vodka. After a brief pause he continued: But notwithstanding glorious traditions, the legacy of our forefathers, notwithstanding the fact of superb military and political preparation, the three Heroes, the Orders of the Red Star, and all the efforts of the respective commanders and political workers, there are isolated shortcomings, although we are maintaining constant, painstaking work on them, that is to say, an unyielding and uncompromising struggle . . . And then what happened happened. Did what happened happen by chance? Both yes and no – a moral code, the great humanism of our ideals, the harmony of domestic and foreign cultures, but in our life there still persist ugly remnants of the past, hostile to socialism, like greed and corruption, the desire to take the most from society and give it nothing in return, mismanagement and waste, drunkenness and hooliganism, bureaucracy and the callous treatment of others, and thus there are isolated irresponsible elements, criminal elements, in fact, that allow themselves physically and morally to humiliate a human being!

I was sitting in the first row, listening. I thought: just maybe, I . . . I still had a year to go before demobilization. I looked at the major's hard face, at his small, strong hands, at the faces of the staff officers who were listening with satisfaction to the major, and I thought: No.

I didn't stand up and I didn't say anything. When the major had finished the staff officers stood up and spoke along the same lines as Akimov. After dinner the officers flew back to Kabul in helicopters. The veterans connected to the desertion of the young soldier were imprisoned. But for some reason the remaining old-timers did not listen to reason and continued physically and morally to humiliate the kids.

*

'Fedya, really, it's too much,' Marina said when she handed the manuscript back.

'You think so too? Strange. But it's only half true. It was actually much worse.'

'And why "Oratorio"?'

'Nothing to do with music. It comes from the word "orator".'

'That's what I thought.'

'Marina, I've been waiting half a week now for your article,' the director Louisa – Liza said.

'I'll get it to you today,' Marina muttered, and bent down over her papers.

'Your material is late too, Fedya.'

'Message received,' said Pryadilnikov, picking up his pen.

He was writing about military instruction and learning aids, about the education of young people's sensibilities . . . traditions . . . precepts . . . patriotism . . . we, youth, long-haired, our desires are straightforward, give us the vaults of heaven! . . . And the mountains were asleep, the herd of green turtles was asleep, it was quiet, warm. But a hatch cover creaked and a second lieutenant hauled himself out of an armoured transport; he yawned, glanced around at the steppe, and froze when he spotted the black cranes; he vanished for a moment, reappeared, carefully climbed out of the machine, and, crouched low to the ground, walked across the steppe with an assault rifle, the guards following him with their eyes, and the birds caught sight of him, stretched their necks, stiffened, the lieutenant dropped onto one knee, raised the rifle butt to his shoulder, hunched his head, aimed, the birds ran off, bobbing up and down and flapping their wings, the flock took to the air, a pale red burst shot over the steppe and cut into the black flock. The guards watched in silence. It was Pryadilnikov's first operation, he was scared, not sure if, when he felt the crack of bullets around his feet or the whistle of shrapnel over his head, he would keep his composure and behave like a hardened soldier; he was afraid he would make a fool of himself and run away from the battlefield or something as shameful; he recalled all those hardened heroes from films and books but it didn't help, he felt sick, he had lost his appetite and needed to piss all the time, but the raid was taking place peacefully, without any shooting, and only on this morning of the second day did Pryadilnikov hear any shooting or see any death: the second lieutenant dropped down to one knee, hunched his head, aimed, and a tracer burst, tracer . . . tracer . . . tracer . . . Where did I want to go this morning? Pryadilnikov thought. I dreamed of something and wanted to go. What could I have dreamed about? Tracer . . . trr . . . aa . . . ss.

'Louisa,' Pryadilnikov said. 'Something isn't right with me at all.'

'Fyodor.' Louisa looked at him severely. 'Don't be a jellyfish. Pull yourself together. It has to be done today.'

Pryadilnikov lit a cigarette.

'Well, children,' Louisa said. 'I'm off to the library. We haven't got the book here. Behave yourselves.' She walked over to the mirror on the wall, arranged her short dark hair, put lipstick on her large, pouty lips, took two steps backwards to see the reflection of her legs, looked herself over, smiled to herself, and left.

Marina and Pryadilnikov were sitting at their desks and writing in silence. From time to time Marina would cast glances at Pryadilnikov. He seemed especially sick and exhausted today, and she wanted to feed him. She wanted to take his cigarettes away from him. She wanted to mend the faded, tattered, frayed cuffs of his jeans. She wanted to rub his lame leg.

The door opened.

'Oh! Pardon, pardon,' Gostyev cried out, then vanished.

Some ten minutes passed and there was a knock on the door.

'Yes!' Pryadilnikov called out.

The door opened a crack. The Zavsepech's eyeglasses were glowing white in the doorway. He seemed to be acting strangely.

'May I? I'm not bothering you too much?'

'Please,' Pryadilnikov mumbled, puzzled. What did he want?

'Excuse me, of course,' the Zavsepech said as he came in. 'Of course I understand humour, but . . . there's a time for fun and a time for work.' He looked intently at Marina. 'Good day, young person.'

Marina raised her eyes from her article, glanced at him, blushed, and hastily said, 'Good day.'

The Zavsepech turned towards Pryadilnikov. 'And good day to you, veteran, so to speak.'

'We salute you, so to speak.'

The Zavsepech stared blankly at him: a little mockery from the puppy, eh?

'Might I please sit down?' the Zavsepech asked with mock humility.

'Sit, sit, please, for the love of the God who doesn't exist. Would you like some coffee? We'll make some.'

'Please, no. But thank you. You're writing?'

'Yes.'

'Business as usual, the bureau writing, ha, ha. And what, may I ask, is stirring your young hearts just now?'

'My young heart is racked with grief about imperfections in military and patriotic instruction in the city schools. And her young heart by drunkenness and all the other rashes and pimples from the bourgeois past that have arisen in the body of Soviet studentdom.'

'The little students are drinking?'

Marina nodded.

'Good-for-nothings. But not the overwhelming majority?'

'No, no,' Pryadilnikov answered instead of Marina. 'It's atypical. She's describing a specific case. But Soviet students in general are very very.'

The Zavsepech narrowed his eyes. 'What?'

'Nothing. Just very very. Very very and most most.'

'You criticise everything, Pryadilnikov,' the Zavsepech said with a smile. 'Always with dark glasses planted firmly on your nose, always looking at the world from your trench . . . Is your medal repaired?'

'Yes. Only there's a new problem: the colour's chipped off, it has to be repainted, but I can't find the right enamel anywhere.'

'However,' the Zavsepech said, frowning, 'you might think a bit before talking that way about a state decoration.'

'We journalists talk first and think later, in the thick of it.'

'And that's bad! Very bad! I would advise you to think first. Thoroughly. Tho-rough-ly!' the Zavsepech exclaimed in an irritated voice. 'Isn't it time to be serious? Why is it all such a big farce with you, d'you hear me? Why be such a clown? I don't like that style at all. Granted, the youth press is a bit easygoing, which can be seen in the attitude of the editorial employees, but not to this degree! Journalism is a serious matter. There has to be a sense of responsibility. If you're not capable of feeling a sense of responsibility, then it's worth thinking about it very thoroughly: is this really the place for me?'

'I think about that all the time, Demyan Vasilevich: is this the place for you? That's what I ask myself: Fedya, is this the place for you?'

The Zavsepech fixed his eyes on Pryadilnikov. Marina smiled

a startled smile and turned away towards the window. The smile didn't escape the Zavsepech.

'Where's the editor?' he asked quietly. He was still in control of himself.

'Probably in his office, I don't know,' Pryadilnikov answered.

'Call him in.'

Pryadilnikov looked darkly at the Zavsepech and repeated: 'He's probably in his office.'

The Zavsepech stared at Pryadilnikov.

'Just a moment,' Marina said, and stood up.

But the Zavsepech had risen too and left without another word.

'You've lost your mind,' Marina said.

'Yes, I have,' Pryadilnikov agreed, and lit a cigarette.

Very soon the Zavsepech's voice could be heard from the other side of the door: 'There, Yegor Petrovich, there, just look at those jokers. Eh? After all it's an editorial office, not a circus. And what if it wasn't me but a visitor who'd seen it? What would he have thought of us? They write at the level of second-year high-school students, but their ambitions – oh! oh-ho-ho! You've let your gadflies get out of hand, Yegor Petrovich. No seriousness at all, no political maturity at all, just sarcasm. The Party and the government, you understand, have shown their concern for that so-called veteran of yours, they've given him a car, they've given him an apartment – he's living off the fat of the land. What did you and I have at his age? Eh? And he mocks and scoffs at everything, he's always playing, you understand, the victim. He laughs at his state decoration! And so on and so on. We have to undertake a review. For a long time I've closed my eyes to your gadflies – but that's enough. You've collected, you understand, all sorts of underripe buffoons – clowns, you understand. But there are, we have at our disposal competent, serious journalists.

There are. They've been with the provincial papers for years. Experienced, mature. He writes like a dog, but his ambition – oh! oh-ho-ho! And on top of that I have some information . . .'

The door was thrown open and the knob slammed into the wall.

'Look at him!' the Zavsepech demanded.

The editor glanced wearily at Pryadilnikov.

'Just look at his face. His place is in a drying-out clinic. I have verified proof.'

Pryadilnikov was leaning back on his stool, smoking and staring at the ceiling.

The Zavsepech couldn't stand the sight: he turned around abruptly and stalked off down the corridor. As soon as his steps had faded away everyone who worked in the area drifted into the student youth section, even the old typist. The editor sat down, took off his glasses, wiped them with his handkerchief, and lit a cheap cigarette.

'What on earth got into Demyan Vasilevich?' the grey-haired typist asked.

The editor showed her a sheet of paper. There was a heart pierced by an arrow drawn on it, with the words: 'Love break – 10.00–10.15.'

'It was hanging on the door,' the editor explained, 'and then he walked past.'

The old woman pulled out her glasses, held them up to her eyes, and looked at the piece of paper. She livened up and glanced at Marina with interest. The director of the Komsomol life section stretched his lips into a deadened smile.

'Is this your work, numskull?' the editor asked Gostyev, despondently.

Gostyev lowered his eyes.

'Gostyev, we're going to have to do something about this,' said the director of the Komsomol life section, a man in his thirties who drank a lot in his youth but had recovered from the fatal passion five years before. He didn't drink, was healthy and energetic, but for five years he had been smiling that dead Jesuit smile.

'I can explain,' Gostyev said. 'I have an idea what this is all about.'

'Shouldn't expect much of fools,' the editor muttered.

'I suspect,' Gostyev said, 'that it wasn't the joke. Think about it, a heart's a heart. It's not a naked woman or anything. I think I know what this is all about. It's something else.'

'I'm dropping everything, fuck it all, and I'm moving to my in-laws, in the countryside, where I'm going to raise mad bulls,' the editor announced.

'To put it simply,' Gostyev continued, 'the Zavsepech has feelings for Marina. The old man has a complex.'

'I'm sick of you and your psychoanalysis,' Marina said, and left the room.

'It's Freud, not me.'

'Well, and you? Why do you always have to shoot your mouth off? Why did you have to rattle on at him as if you were manning a machine-gun? Fyodor – blue pools – you ought to hold your tongue,' the editor said.

'I got sick of commanders and Zampolits in the army.'

The editor looked out of the window at the sunlit street.

'In the country. Steaming milk, fishing,' he muttered. 'Rabbit-hunting, a little bathhouse, a kitchen garden, a herd of mad bulls – bliss.'

Towards evening Pryadilnikov's head was roaring with tobacco and military-patriotic sentences like a stove full of pine logs, the only difference being that only he could hear it. He put the last touch to the article and handed it in. Louisa kissed him on the forehead. And he asked her for some money. But you said you had money, she replied. I'm just very shy, he said. And what will you buy? Milk and bread. Really? I swear. Well, just make sure it isn't anything inflammable. Yes ma'am, I promise. He took the ten-rouble note and asked: Allow me to kiss your hand, mademoiselle? Better kiss Marina's. Don't be a fool, Marina said to Pryadilnikov, who was heading towards her. Ah, Marina, you're no maker of your own happiness, Louisa said.

At ten to six everyone got ready to go home.

'Maestro, what plans do you have for the evening?' Pryadilnikov inquired of the Beard.

The Beard turned his sad, beautiful eyes to him and said in a melancholy voice: I'm going home. Come on, let's go to my place for a little bit, Pryadilnikov pressed. My wife will run back to her mother's again, the Beard answered; I'll pass, but go and ask Gostyev there. I'm sick to death of Gostyev, said Pryadilnikov. Well, I don't know then, but I'll pass, the Beard replied, then picked up his case, beat a hasty retreat, and even forgot to say good-bye to everyone.

'Fyodor! Did my ears deceive me?' Louisa shouted out.

'It was a joke.'

'Well look here.' Louisa threatened him with her fist. She said good-bye, then left.

Marina was slowly arranging pieces of paper on her desk. Pryadilnikov picked up the receiver, dialled the number with his index finger. No answer. He drummed his fingers on the phone and dialled another number. Silence, or rather, long rings. The pine logs were groaning and splitting, the pile of cinders crackling. Pryadilnikov rubbed his temples with his index fingers. He tried the two numbers again, hung up, said 'Later' to Marina, and disappeared out of the door.

Marina sat there, not moving, looking at the door.

*

He took the lift down, passed by the militiamen without looking at them, went out onto the steps, limped between the Parthenon-style columns, walked to his armoured car, unlocked the door, and climbed in. 'Where to?' he asked the car.

Have to remember last night's dream, and then it would be clear where to go.

Pryadilnikov wrinkled his forehead. No, it was useless. He started the engine and drove out into the street. The armoured car started to glide leisurely through the autumn streets. Black birds settled onto the steppe. Then they flew away again, Pryadilnikov was thinking. Black birds settled onto the steppe. The mountains were asleep, the herd of green turtles was asleep, and it was quiet, warm, there were white flowers, the cranes landed, it was quiet and warm, there were white flowers, the flowers were white, whiteflowers, cranewomen, tank-turtles . . . shit!

He braked by the liquor shop.

'Any wine?' he asked a shabby-looking man in sports slacks and a blue jersey.

'Just vodka, but they say there's some wine at Jubilee. Mind taking me too?'

'Sure.' The man climbed in next to him.

They stopped in front of the shop called 'Jubilee'. Can I tag along with you, the man asked. Pryadilnikov shook his head. Bastard, the man said, and got out of the car. Pryadilnikov climbed out after he did.

Two men were loitering by the shop door. They stopped a boy walking past and said something to him. The boy unhesitatingly reached into his pocket, gave them some change, and went on his way. The two spotted Pryadilnikov. One of them, jolly, brown-eyed, strode over towards him, smiled, and held out his hand:

Hello! Pryadilnikov mechanically returned the handshake. The stranger squeezed his hand: Give me something, little brother, for a bit of wine, quick, quick. Pryadilnikov was no miser, but that 'quick, quick' rubbed him the wrong way and he replied, pulling his hand back, 'I'm a bum.'

He bought wine and cigarettes in the store and went back out into the street. Hey, bum, why don't we go and have a little chat in the bushes, the jolly brown-eyed one said. No time for that. Come on, Silver, come on, let's go. But Pryadilnikov kept walking towards his armoured car. Give it up, the second said to the first, it's a sin to beat up cripples. Pryadilnikov gritted his teeth but didn't stop. He opened the car door, got in, laid the plastic bag with the bottles in it on the seat, turned the key. The engine came to life. Pryadilnikov glanced out of the window. The two were still loitering. What a lousy day, Pryadilnikov thought, and turned off the engine. He found his penknife in the mess in the car, pulled at the blade with his fingernail, and drew it out of its handle. He put the open knife in his pocket. He unsealed the pack, took out a cigarette, lit it, and climbed out of the car.

'What do you want, Silver?' the jolly one asked, surprised.

'Come on, let's go,' said Pryadilnikov.

'Ha! The little bull's blood is up!' the jolly one exclaimed.

'We were joking, stay alive,' the second one said appeasingly.

'Let's go,' Pryadilnikov repeated.

'Listen, Silver, you'd better get away from here,' advised the second one, 'or you'll be limping on both legs.'

'Hello, kids!'

All three turned around. Louisa.

'Hello, pussycat, if you're serious,' the jolly one answered quickly, looking Louisa over.

'Out buying milk, Fedya?'

Pryadilnikov said nothing.

'Problems, kids?'

'Endless,' the jolly one replied. 'Never enough.'

'There,' said Louisa, taking a rouble coin out of her purse.

'It isn't a fake?'

'So, any more problems?' Louisa asked.

'That's everything. No problems,' the jolly one replied.

'Let's get home,' Louisa said crisply, and pulled Pryadilnikov by the arm.

'You're late, your man is already packing it in.'

Louisa dragged Pryadilnikov away.

'Not bad, the little filly,' the jolly one said.

'Come on,' the second one said, and headed into the shop.

The armoured car was rolling down the street. You really picked a pair to tangle with, Louisa said. Pryadilnikov didn't answer. You really picked the right ones to tangle with, they would have killed you, don't you know what kind of brutes they were? No doubt they both had knives in their pockets. Criminal mugs, they'd cut a sheep's throat or a man's with just as much pleasure. And prison is home to them. So, are you going to drink all by yourself? No, Pryadilnikov answered, there are two fellows I can always count on, classmates. Louisa didn't say anything for a moment. Can I keep you company? Pryadilnikov glanced at her. Sure, keep me company. Louisa smiled: I was joking, my husband's waiting for me, he's jealous as a bull. Why would bulls be jealous? I don't know, the word just popped into my head. Keep me company, Pryadilnikov said again. Louisa's eyes sparkled. It would be better if you asked Marina. Marina? Why Marina? Why, why – open your eyes and look at her, that's why. So, my place then? Pryadilnikov asked. You're so cool, Louisa said, rolling her eyes languidly. Next time, Fedya, today I can't.

The armoured car came to a halt outside Louisa's building.

Louisa picked up her handbag and opened the car door. Pryadilnikov looked at her sullenly. She lingered for a moment. Pryadilnikov looked at her. She said, quietly and firmly, 'Next time,' and got out.

He didn't go to his classmates. He didn't feel like it any more. He would have to talk, listen, smile, and after a whole day of that he was tired of talking, listening, smiling. His tongue was heavy, his ears were hurting, and his flesh had turned to rubber from smiling. It was good to live alone: if he wanted company he could invite someone over, and if he wanted to be alone he wouldn't invite anyone. The worst thing about the army was that there had been nowhere to hide. Even in the latrines there was always someone grunting.

Only one person. Only one person had been always welcome, night and day, on duty or at home, when things were bad or good, one, only one, who could understand anything from just half a word . . .

The recce company went out often. Yes, too often; they put on their combat gear and sneakers – like hikers – and slipped away from camp at night, and would return, just as suddenly, two or three days later, covered with dust, unshaven; the recce company would vanish and I would begin to wait, going to their tents every day to find out whether or not they were back. Then the company would return; I'd go to their tents, see the dirt-crusted boys cleaning their weapons; I'd crane my neck and try to spot the long, hook-nosed face, and sometimes I'd see it off in the distance, sometimes not; I would walk up to the boys: Well, lads, how did it go? They: The usual. Or: Lousy. And they would add: He went off to the weapons depot, or to the baths, or somewhere else. I would find him and ask: Like a smoke? He: Yes! I: But the Minister of Health warns against it. He: I want to be a human being, and one learned old man has said: A human being is a featherless bipedal creature that smokes! I: Well then, take this present from Africa. I would give him a pack of cigarettes, much prized in the army – Soviet or Bulgarian cigarettes, but our ritual was: A present from Africa is a present from Africa! Beyond the firing range was a hill that had provided marble to build the baths, storehouses, and toilets. The marble was white with sea-green stripes. Sometimes we managed to escape there; we would settle down among the sunlit slabs, the snow-white slabs. The snow-white slabs, the sun shining, the marble painful to look at – he opens a book and reads out loud from Baudelaire, Rimbaud the wanderer, Verlaine, Bunin, Blok, Yevtushenko. I don't read because I'm awful at it, but he reads wonderfully, he reads wonderfully because he writes poems too. He reads, I lie back on the warm rocks, smoke a cheap *makhorka* cigarette; I look down at the camp, the steppe, at the distant southern mountains, they say it's already Pakistan there, they say that cedars grow there, and to the west are the Iskapol mountains, was it the Greeks who named them that? Alexander the Great waged war here once . . . The Iskapol mountains are bare, their peaks snowy; I look at the Iskapol mountains, at the cedar-covered mountains to the south, and far away on the steppe I see a caravan: tiny camels, delicate white marching figures . . . But more often no one would be moving anywhere on the hot, dusty, hard, bare land. 'I am a man, like God I am condemned to know the anguish of all nations and all times.' I lie back on the warm, brilliant rocks, looking at the sun through a chip of white marble with a sea-green stripe, and I tell him that we should be living on the shore of some ocean. He shuts the book, takes the translucent chip from me, looks at the sun through the sea-green wave, and agrees that we should live by the ocean when we get out of the army. Every now and then he reads his own poems, and that's better than Baudelaire, or Blok, or Yevtushenko. The recce company often went out on raids, too often; the company would drive away and each time I would try to find out whether or not it had returned. Then I would walk over and see, in the distance, the blackened boys in their sun-faded fatigues: Hi, how did it go? The usual, and he's in his tent. Like a smoke? But the Minister of Health, take this present from Africa, you haven't read anything of yours for a long time. I'm not writing, nothing comes at all, Villon was a hopeless debauchee but he still wrote, and I'm not that hopeless yet but nothing – or am I already hopeless? Don't worry, you'll still turn out an armour-piercing poem and the masters will all weep with envy. Hi, how did it go? Fine, and he's at the weapons depot. Hi, how did it go? Badly, and he's in the yard of the medical unit. The yard of the medical unit, at its centre a canvas tent on four iron poles planted in the ground, and under the tent three humped sheets. A medic captain: Hey, don't go poking around there. I have to, captain, my comrade's there. Well go then. I drew the sheet away from the face, looked, left, came back, stuck a pack of cigarettes under the sheet, then stood there in the middle of the yard. It was hot and flies were flying over the sheets; I was standing in the sun in the middle of the scorching medical unit yard, the sheets were white under the tent, the yard was describing slow circles, rhythmic circles, in its centre were the white sheets, motionless, dead sheets, sheets of stone, the yard was spinning around, the medical unit and the marble latrines were spinning around, the latrines stank of disinfectant, the sun was smeared with sticky brown disinfectant, the fetid liquid was running into the sky, spilling down to the earth, and flies were flying around the sheets: to and fro, fro and to . . .

Pryadilnikov poured from the bottle into his glass and thought: I'm sick of the editorial office . . . He drank the glass,

ate an apple and a piece of cheese. He lit a cigarette and thought:
I'm tired of the colonnaded building, I don't want to see the
Zavsepech. And I'm bored with that kennel. But there's a good
place somewhere. Cigarette smoke was curling coyly in front of
his face. Too bad that Louisa didn't come. Louisa, Liza, liz-liz-liz.
The black things landed . . .

The birds with long white necks beat their wings soundlessly,
stretched out their legs, alighted on the earth. There were white
flowers on the steppe – lumps of soapsuds floating low to the
ground. The company was asleep in its armoured transports. The
guards saw the flock. It was early in the morning, warm and
quiet. The birds landed, lowered their huge wings, cleaned their
feathers with their beaks, and, peering around, wandered among
the grass and flowers. They had white necks and red crowns, and
every now and then they would stand still, turn their heads
towards the column, and stare at it. The guards didn't budge and
the birds probably mistook them for pillars, and the armoured
transports for shining green turtles. The white-necked birds
were striding back and forth on the steppe, they were black, the
steppe was green, the hills and the herd of green turtles were
asleep, there was a crimson light in the sky to the east. The
guards looked at one another and smiled.

A hatch cover creaked and a second lieutenant hauled himself
out of one of the transports; he yawned, glanced around at the
steppe, and froze when he spotted the birds. He vanished for a
moment, reappeared, climbed out of the machine, and, crouched
low to the ground, walked across the steppe with an assault rifle
in his hands. The guards followed him with their eyes. The birds
caught sight of the lieutenant, stretched their necks, stiffened.
The lieutenant raised the rifle, dropped to one knee, set the rifle
butt against his shoulder, hunched his head, aimed. The birds ran
off, flapping their wings. The flock took to the air. A pale red

burst shot over the steppe and cut into the flock. One of the guards raised his assault rifle to his shoulder and fired a short burst without taking aim. A second and a third grabbed their rifles too and started shooting. And Pryadilnikov raised his rifle to his shoulder and fired two long bursts of tracer. One and two and three and four. One! Two! Three! Four!

Sleepy soldiers leaped, weapons in hand, out of the armoured transports.

The cranes flew away. A few birds lay motionless on the steppe. Two, their wings broken, were flailing in the grass. The guards ran over, struck them with their rifle-butts, and dragged them by their legs towards the column. The lieutenant and the soldiers bent down over the tattered birds, looking for wounds and arguing about where the bullets had entered and exited. The captain appeared, furious. He yelled at the lieutenant and the guards and promised to give them all three days in the cooler for the false alarm. The lieutenant nodded towards the rising sun and said that reveille had been called on time. The captain didn't answer.

The soldiers climbed down onto the steppe and, yawning, urinated while watching the wine-coloured sun rise over the green earth. Then they had breakfast – biscuits, cold tea, lumps of sugar, and canned fish in tomato sauce. The lieutenant was talking loudly about how he hunted geese in the tundra, grey, plump geese, delicious, fat, tender geese. The soldiers were swallowing wet, red pieces of fish and listening to him.

He had dreamed it again. Pryadilnikov woke up in the morning and the first thing he did was try to recall the dream. He dreamed of something yellow, dry, rustling, rounded. Yellow, dry, rustling, rounded, yellow, rustling, yellow – the mountain!

The mountain! Pryadilnikov got up and went to wash. He

cupped cold water in his hands and splashed his face with it. The mountain! The mountain in autumn.

He washed, dried his face with a towel, and went into the kitchen for some tea, strong tea, bitter, hot, sharp, dark, divine tea. On the mountain. Fifteen years ago there had been a mountain. Sharp, cherry-coloured, no, peat-coloured tea. Pryadilnikov wiped his sweaty face with his hand and poured a second cup. On the mountain. How could he have forgotten? There had been a mountain, and a rabbit. The rabbit had been white, with crimson eyes. He had given a rusty German bayonet in exchange for it to a small boy who lived in a one-family wooden house. The rabbit moved into their seventh-floor apartment. It lived in a suitcase under his writing-desk. The rabbit was like a dog. When the boy came home from school the rabbit would leap out of the suitcase and hop along the walls to the boy across the room. The boy fed it cabbage and crusts of bread and carried it against his chest when he went for walks. His parents called the rabbit a pest and threatened to throw it outside or roast it in the oven with potatoes. The boy would say to the rabbit: Soon we'll run away. He wanted to run away into the woods with the rabbit, build a hut, and live off rabbit-grass, nuts, and mushrooms. When the boy was given a D one day he showed the exercise book to the rabbit and said: There, you see, it's terrible to be a human. The rabbit twitched its ears in agreement. His father had come home in the evening. He looked at the exercise book and gave the boy a hiding. Sitting in its suitcase and hearing the wails of its master and friend, the rabbit knew for certain that it was better to be a rabbit. After the beating the boy sat by his window. The rabbit crept up to him and began to lick his toenails. He liked that for some reason, licking toenails – could salt gather there from when the boy walked around?

His father said: Another D or a C and the rabbit goes. On the very next day the boy was given a D even though he had learned the whole lesson – he hadn't been able to answer out of sheer fright. He came home, put a blanket, bread, a little knife, salt, and matches into a backpack, hid the rabbit against his chest, reached the station by tram, climbed into a train to the city outskirts, saw a deserted stop through the window, and got out. He found an oak-covered mountain among the fields and spent two days there. During the second night the rabbit vanished. In the morning some peasants out mushroom-hunting found the young boy. The rabbit had no doubt sensed that people would come in the morning. And it had taken off. And it had done the right thing. Maybe to this day it's still free, if it hasn't been eaten by foxes. But the young boy hadn't sensed anything, he hadn't taken off, God only knows what was done to him.

On the mountain, on the mountain, on the mountain.

He put a tea kettle, two blankets, sugar, tea, and bread into a backpack and drove out of the city.

After yesterday's binge his head was spinning, his hands shaking, and his heart beating erratically. Pryadilnikov was sweating heavily.

He drove along the highway south for half an hour. He decided it was time and turned off onto a country road. The sand-coloured armoured car started to rock over the potholes.

There, the housing estate. The railway. Fifteen years before he had spotted this estate from the window of the city train. The train had stopped here. Moved on. There had been another stop, and another. He had climbed out at the third. Or the fourth.

The armoured car clambered up a hill. Beyond the railway Pryadilnikov could make out hills and stands of trees. The mountain had to be somewhere around there. The armoured car crossed the railway and sailed onto bare grey fields covered with cobwebs.

The sand-coloured armoured car rumbled over the fields under a high empty sky.

There weren't any mountains anywhere. Maybe it had never existed. Maybe he had dreamed it. And the white rabbit. And everything else.

His mouth was dry. His heart was beating too hard now, knocking against his shoulder-blade. There were ponds and swamps, but no clean water anywhere. He would have to head towards some village.

The car skirted a stand of trees. The houses of a village began to appear in silhouette straight ahead. Pryadilnikov drove a bit further towards the village, then changed his mind and swung the armoured car round. He didn't want to see people. It could have been peasants from this village who had gone out for mushrooms fifteen years before, caught the young boy on the mountain, and brought him to the militia.

His mouth was dry and bitter.

But had there been water on the mountain? No, not on the mountain. In a little gully, in the bushes. Yes, there's a little gully below the mountain . . . A spring there.

Just before evening Pryadilnikov realized that he wouldn't find it.

He pressed on the brake pedal and the armoured car came to a stop. Pryadilnikov got out.

The sun was shining red and it was already hanging on the forested horizon.

Pryadilnikov looked around.

The land was flat in every direction. Green stands of trees everywhere. Red maples here and there. It was warm. Have to remember, Pryadilnikov thought, have to remember everything clearly. He sat down on the ground, his face to the sun.

*

And so there was a rabbit, white, with crimson eyes, that loved water-melon rinds. And then the two of them ran away. A train to the city outskirts brought them south. After an hour, most likely, they got out. A railway stop.

He walked along a road. Fields all around. He saw the mountain. Swung towards it. It was yellow. Clusters on the lingonberry bushes were glowing a dull red below the mountain. The lingon nourished him with its fragrant berries. On the mountain were yellow maples and oaks. Acorns were tumbling from the oaks. The acorns fell into russet ferns. He took off his cloth cap and stood under the biggest oak. The oak dropped a hard acorn onto the top of his head. It was funny. The rabbit was cautiously getting used to the smells. White in the russet ferns. We're going to live here. We'll build our hut over there. And that aspen will make a great spear to fight off wolves with. Acorns were falling. Everything was warm. Fat thrushes and bright jays were flying in and out of the trees. In the grass were boletus mushrooms. Full, yellow autumn. And not scared at all. The rabbit next to him. The lingonberry like a human being. The bush not quite human. But almost. Go on, I'll feed you with my berries, go o-o-on.

He took a load of hay from a stack in a field. He slept on the hay, covering himself with the blanket. He held the rabbit against his chest so it wouldn't get cold or scared. It was scary at night even though that auntie with her berries was somewhere close by. At night the moon shone. The leaves flew. They dropped, white in the moonlight, and he dreamed that it was snow falling, that snowflakes were settling on his face. He woke up and saw that it was leaves. Winter is still far off, and I'm still hoping to build a hut, warm and solid.

The morning was warm. The September sun shining in the sky. Yellow leaves were falling, yellow leaves quivering in the trees, yellow leaves lying on the blanket, the ground carpeted with yellow leaves, and down below, in the swamp, were yellow birches. He wandered around the mountain, came across the spring in the little gully, collected a panful of water. He made kasha. The rabbit breakfasted on a slab of bread. The rabbit hopped up the mountain and returned. The lingonberry watched from below. A magpie landed. It perched on a maple, examined the young boy and the rabbit, croaked 'Watch it!' It flew off, returned soon after with three friends, and all of them fixed their black eyes on the young boy and the rabbit. He threw a stick at them and they cried, in chorus, 'Watch it!' Then they flew away. Mice raced up and down the mountain. The mountain was rustling, the yellow, rustling mountain.

The jagged horizon had already cut off half the solar disc before the man sitting on the road by his car heard the flapping of wings. Shadows descended from above. They were black birds. They stretched out their legs and settled to the ground. The birds folded their wings. They had long necks with a white stripe from their beaks to their breasts and patches of red on their small heads. The birds paced around in the dry grass, pecking at its flowerlets with their beaks and picking the seeds from the ground. He put down his assault rifle, stood up, and walked away. He slowly climbed down the mountain. He smoothly descended from the mountain. He was walking downwards, not making a sound. The white rabbit was hopping in front of him. The birds spotted them and froze.

They didn't fly away. The big black birds were waiting, with their heads turned towards him.